Criminal Connection

Misha Ray

Published by Twisted Heart Press, LLC
Criminal Connection
Misha Ray
2018
Published by Twisted Heart Press, LLC

Edited by Genevieve Scholl
Formatted by Genevieve Scholl
Cover by Misha Ray

Books by Misha Ray

Paranormal Ménage Erotica:

Breeder of the Pack (Moon Valley Breeders 1)

Breeder to the Pack (Moon Valley Breeders 2)

Breeder for the Pack (Moon Valley Breeders 3)

Breeder to the Whole Pack (Moon Valley Breeders 4)

Paranormal Ménage Erotic Romance:

Her Heart's Desire

Wed to the Shifters

Chapter One

Officer Flora Grumio was tired. She was to the bones, out of her head tired. But sleep was hours away. Instead, she sat parked outside the house of one Dannon Michaels, Incubus and sex on a fucking stick.

She'd been on this case for one week and already she was bored. And turned on. And, honestly, a little pissed. What she was supposed to be catching him doing, she didn't know. So far, everything she'd witnessed Dannon participate in was completely legal. Hell. She probably did more lawbreaking than this monster of a man.

And there he was.

Dannon Michaels sauntered from his house, his jeans encasing powerful legs, the cotton t-shirt hugging all the right places, his aviators covering what she knew were beautiful brown eyes. He hadn't shaved in a while, but damn, that beard just added to the rugged sexiness. And that long hair blowing in the breeze like some romance book cover...

Yeah; she seriously needed to get laid. How was she supposed to be around him and not want him? It was in her fucking blood. He was the male opposite of her species. Once an Incubus and Succubus were locked in a room, someone would be screaming out with orgasm. She just wished it were her.

"You coming?" Dannon called out, waving his hand at her.

He knew she'd been tailing him. How could he not? If she could sense him from out here, no doubt he could sense her just as well.

Lifting her hand in a flirty little wave and grumbling every name she could think of under her breath, Flora started her little Audi and fought the urge to flip him off as Dannon roared past her on his Harley. He had to be doing something to afford a machine so big and shiny, but as of yet, no one could figure out what. He sure as hell wasn't working. Because if Flora wasn't planted outside of every single place he went, someone else was. There was literally no time when Dannon didn't have a babysitter—er, surveillance from the St. Louis Paranormal Police Department.

Following the sexy Incubus, Flora grabbed her phone from the center console and hit her boss's number. "Yeah?" Chief Jane Jarbo answered.

"It's me. Still nothing. Following Dannon now. Heading…" She shifted to the side to see past Dannon's large body. He turned the bike on to Main St. "East on Main Street."

"Moore will be spelling you in two hours. Stop sounding so fucking bored," Chief Jarbo said, a soft chuckle working from her mouth to irritate Flora's ear.

"You realize we're not going to get anything on him, right? How long have we been searching?"

"You've only been on this case for a week. I've been dealing with his ass for six months."

"Kind of my point. Six months and nothing. Any chance he's actually clean?" she asked, shaking her head as Dannon pulled his bike on to the highway heading toward East St. Louis where she knew the fucker was going straight to a strip club.

"Where's his money coming from? Where are the people who crossed him?"

"They deserved it," Flora said, hitting the button to roll up her window as she pushed the gas pedal harder.

"Doesn't matter. We have laws for a reason. These disappearances keep up and the humans will start their bullshit again and try to keep us more restrained."

"Yeah. Good luck to them."

The paranormal beings of the planet—or Others, as the humans called them—had come out of hiding twelve years ago. It had taken a few of those years to get the humans used to their presence and not constantly try to stake anyone who was in the Other category through the heart. Humans watched too many fucking movies. Eventually, every city formed their own departments of Paranormal

Police to keep their own kind under control since the human police couldn't handle the strength and speed of so many of the Others.

Just as Flora guessed, Dannon pulled his motorcycle in to the parking lot of Roxy's Delight and killed the engine. The bastard sat on the machine and waited for her to park next to him.

"I've got to go. Looks like Dannon wants to chat before paying girls to shake their tits in his face. Two hours. I want to go home," Flora said, ending the call and pulling her seat belt off. "Could you be any more clichéd?" she asked Dannon after she rolled her window down.

A smile pulled those full lips up. "Want to join me?" he asked.

Okay. That she hadn't expected. "In there?" He nodded. "Why the hell would I want to go to a strip club?" Although, feeding from the lust sure to be pouring from the men in there would definitely sate some of her need.

He pulled his sunglasses off and hooked them on the front of his t-shirt. "Because you're no different than me," he said, his voice calm as he studied her. Those damn eyes were boring in to her and making certain body parts quiver.

"I like dick, thank you."

That crooked smile was back and now Dannon's eyes were moving as if he could see her body through the steel of her car. "You know where I am if you change your mind. Or you could just sit out here for two hours." The bastard could hear Flora talking to her Chief through her closed window. Of course he could. His hearing was just as sensitive as hers.

He shrugged, threw his leg over the bike, and sauntered into the club. Damn. His ass looked good in those jeans. Had she not already known what he was, she would've guessed him as a shifter by his size.

Dannon looked at her over his shoulder one more time before pulling the door open and disappearing inside. With a sigh, Flora leaned her head against the seat and stared through the windshield. After a few minutes of staring at absolutely nothing, she turned her head to check out Dannon's motorcycle. There was no way that thing cost him less than fifteen grand. What did it feel like to ride one of those? Did it vibrate and rumble between his legs?

Hell. She wished he'd rumble between her legs. Would that be against department policy? Was there something in her handbook against fraternizing with possible subjects of supposed crimes? Because, honestly, since there were no bodies, there was no proof of murder or any other crimes.

"Fuck," she growled out, hitting her head against the seat a couple of times. Two hours of sitting here while horny humans came and went. This was so fucking boring. She wanted to make a difference, catch the bad guys, save lives. Instead, she got Dannon duty.

Turning her head again, she stared at his motorcycle then looked up at the club. There was a guy standing at the door looking out into the parking lot. He glanced in her direction, turned and said something over his shoulder, looked at her one more time, then stepped back inside. Oh, hell no. Was he alerting Dannon that she was still there? Was he warning him or something? Maybe all this time he'd been slipping out the back door of the various places he led her to.

Not today, asshole.

Rolling her window up, she pushed the door open, hit the lock button, and stomped across the parking lot and yanked the door open. The scents of lust, cigarettes, stale beer, and sweat assailed her nose. Every club seemed to smell the same. But after years of waitressing and bartending, she was used to it. It was almost a homey smell.

Letting her eyes adjust, she scanned the room for the big Incubus, spotting his long, brown hair across the club in a corner. The man who'd stepped outside sat next to him in the booth, but far enough away to not seem too intimate. She didn't think Dannon swung both ways, but with their kind, it wasn't exactly unheard of.

As if he could feel her eyes on him, he looked straight at her, a smile tugging at his lips. With a jerk of his head, he invited her over. She crossed the room and stood in front of the table with her arms crossed.

10

"About time," he said. With a wave of his hand, his companion was dismissed. "Sit. Let me buy you a drink."

"I'm on duty," she said, still standing.

"Then I'll buy you a coffee," he said, his smile faltering.

With a sigh, she dropped her arms and scooted in to the booth, keeping a healthy distance between she and Dannon. Every cell in her body screamed to climb onto his lap. Her primal side, that part of her that she was trying so hard to deny and ignore, wanted her to undo his pants and pull his cock free. She wanted to know how big it was, what it looked like, how it tasted.

She desperately needed to feed.

Instead, she secured an irritated and bored look on her face and did her best to avoid his stare. "Are you going to ignore me all night?" he asked. When she glanced at him, his bottom lip was poking out in a pout.

Damn him. She couldn't hide her amusement. Allowing a small smile, she shook her head. "Couldn't you have picked anywhere else?" she asked.

"What? You don't like tits?"

"I already told you. I'm in to dicks."

"So, feed on the lust. I know you haven't fed in hours. I've seen you outside my house all day."

Well, shit. He had a point. Maybe she couldn't drink, but she could drink in the lust pouring from all the horny men watching the women shaking their bare tits and asses on stage. A waitress approached their table, obvious appreciation in her eyes. A low growl trickled up Flora's throat and she coughed to cover it. Where the hell had that come from?

But Dannon hadn't missed it. With a mischievous smile, he turned his attention back to the waitress. "Another Crown and..." He turned to Flora.

"A soda. Coke or Pepsi. Whatever you have," Flora answered.

The waitress never looked at Flora, but she smiled and nodded her head at Dannon before hurrying away to fill their order.

"So, Officer Grumio," Dannon said, his hand on the back of the booth. His fingers grazed the back of her neck and Flora jerked away. He chuckled. "What do you do for fun when you're not following me around?"

She turned to stare at him. "Knit," she lied.

He threw his head back and laughed. "For some reason, I can't picture you with needles and yarn. Now, how about the truth?"

"What does it matter?" she asked, a shiver working up her spine as he twisted a lock of her hair around his index finger. And he had very long fingers. Fingers that just promised naughty things.

"Because you know everything about me and I know nothing about you," he answered honestly. When she looked at him, he looked genuinely interested.

With another of those irritated sighs that he was oh-so-good at pulling from her, she turned and looked out into the club. "My name is Flora. And I like to read."

His eyebrows lifted. "Read? As in books?"

She snorted a laugh. "Well, yeah."

"What kind of books, Flora?" he asked. The sound of her name on his tongue made her clinch her thighs together. He just oozed so much sexuality and power, colliding with the essence of her own kind.

"You'll laugh," she said. Why did she care what he thought?

He held up one hand. "I won't. Promise."

"I like romance books. But those historical ones. Especially ones set in renaissance times."

He nodded, pressing his lips into a thin line. "So, you like to read about the duchess getting her bodice ripped open?"

"You're laughing," she said, unable to even pretend to be mad.

"I am not. I think it's cute."

Cute. Like a puppy. No. She wanted him to think she was sexy. Didn't she? No. Wait. She was a cop and he was a suspect. Or something. Shut up, body. I'm trying to work.

But as Dannon leaned over to whisper in her ear, it was obvious her body was completely ignoring her. "I like your name," he whispered, his lips close to her ear. "It's sweet and sexy. Like you."

"You know nothing about me," she said, but her voice was breathier than she'd intended. Clearing her throat, she pulled back. "You know nothing about me," she repeated more forceful.

"I know you're a sappy romantic. And by the scent rolling from your body, I know you want me."

She turned to gawk at him. Well, that worked to shut her fucking body up. She liked a confident man, but he was just being cocky. Scooting out of the booth, she nodded her head. "My relief will be here in an hour and a half. I'm sure he'll enjoy watching naked chicks with you. See you later," she said.

He narrowed his eyes at her but didn't say anything as she turned and stomped away from him. She barely made it through the door and into the fading sunlight when a strong hand closed around her bicep and jerked her to a stop. When she turned to cuss out whoever dared to touch her, she got an eyeful of Dannon before his mouth slammed down on hers.

Flora pushed at his chest, trying to shove him away. And then her body betrayed her. Going almost limp, she leaned in to him, opening her lips when his tongue swiped at the seam, allowing him to tease her, taste her, tempt her. His dick was hard and pressed against her inner thigh as he pulled them closer together.

And the mother fucker pulled away abruptly, leaving her foggy brained and unsteady on her feet. Holding onto her for another second, he smiled that sexy ass crooked smile of his and turned her toward her car. He actually escorted her across the parking lot, opened her door when she unlocked it, and settled her into her seat before stepping back. "I'll see you later," he said before swinging the door shut.

He walked backward, that smile still plastered on his face. Then he turned and walked back into the club. And she was left with damp panties and a thundering heart, wondering what the hell had just happened.

Dannon knew the pretty cop would eventually join him. He'd felt her every time she arrived to keep an eye on him. She was definitely his favorite and he'd developed a slight crush on the bleach blonde. Oh, it was obvious that wasn't her natural color; she had dark brows and almost silver-white hair. It fit her, though. She was spunky, sassy, and sexy as hell.

He'd planned on letting her leave the building to sit in her car until he'd seen that cocksucker Kian watching her. Dannon didn't know if he was interested in her or in just fucking with him. So instead of risking the vampire prince following her out and doing something to make Dannon have to break a few more laws, he'd made sure to put some kind of claim on her. It would've been better if he could've come on her, but there were too many humans around for him to just bend her over right there in the doorway.

What he hadn't expected was the way his body instantly reacted to her lips. Fuck. He hadn't been that turned on by a woman's lips since he was a kid trying to feel his first set of titties. He was keyed up, his dick straining against the zipper of his jeans, and now all he wanted to do was take her home and keep her there. Keep her safe from harm, whether it be real or just in his head.

"She's cute," Jim said, his eyes on the chick stepping from the stage.

"She's young," he said. The dancer didn't look much older than twenty-one to Jim's forty-four.

"Not her, dumb ass. The cop. That the lady who's been following you around?"

"One of them," Dannon said, his mind on Flora. Even her name made his dick twitch. He had to bury himself in her soon. There was no way around that or his crush would turn into an obsession.

"You could always seduce her and get her on your side. Wouldn't hurt to have some ears and eyes on the inside," Jim said, still watching the young dancer as she made her way through the crowd.

Dannon shook his head, but Jim wasn't paying attention. No. He wouldn't pull her into his shit. In Dannon's head, every single one of those fuckers deserved what they got and society was safer without them walking around, whether he had a hand in or not. But, Flora was a cop. She was the law. And she had a duty to put those who broke that law away or down. Honestly, he'd rather his head be taken than be locked away. He'd go crazy in the pits.

Glancing at his phone, he realized time was ticking by. Flora would be off duty soon and some other prick would take her place. Nah. He wanted to see her one more time before she left for the night.

"I'm out," Dannon said, clapping Jim on the shoulder as he stood.

"See ya," Jim said, now watching a new dancer shake her fake tits.

Dannon had never been in to implants. He liked them soft under his hand. He liked to watch them bounce when he fucked. He had a feeling Flora's would feel like heaven in his hand by the way they jiggled as she walked across the club earlier.

Stepping in to the early evening, he couldn't hide the smile; Flora held her forehead in her hand with her elbow propped on the window. She was frustrated, and he'd done that to her. If only she knew how easy it would be for him to ease that discomfort.

Tapping lightly on the window, Dannon held his hands out in front of him when she jerked her head toward him. "Didn't you feel me coming?" he asked. Even if she hadn't been paying attention and heard him near her car, she should've at least felt his essence beating against hers.

"I was distracted," she said, her tone grumpy, her dark brows pulled together. "What do you want?"

"I'm going home. You might want to call your buddy and tell him not to bother coming here tonight," he said, throwing a leg over his Road King.

He started the engine, watching her expression out of the corner of his eye as it purred and hummed between his legs. She liked it. Maybe he'd offer her a ride someday. But he wanted her to ride his dick first.

As he took various turns, he watched in his side mirror to make sure she was still behind him. And then he was in front of his house, pulling up the driveway. She took her usual spot across the street in front of his neighbor. "Hey," he said, stalking toward her car.

She rolled her window down. "You're awful chatty today," she said, a suspicious frown pulling those dark brows down again.

"Why don't you come in?" And that suspicious look deepened. "You can report in and tell them all about my nefarious living conditions."

A smile ticked at the corner of her lips, but she licked her lips and shook her head. Pulling her phone out, she pushed a number and held it to her ear. "It's me," she said when a female answered. She had to know he could hear both sides of the conversation. "Dannon Michaels has invited me inside of his house."

"Do you think it's safe?" the woman said.

"Would I tell her to call you first if I planned on doing anything to her?" Dannon answered Flora's supervisor. He cocked a brow at Flora and smiled. Oh, he planning on doing things to her, but nothing she wouldn't beg for.

The line went silent for a few seconds then the woman sighed. "Go in, check it out, and call me when you're done, Grumio," the woman said. That had to be the Chief because he couldn't imagine a woman like Flora took commands from anyone.

But she was about to learn how to become submissive.

"Will do," Flora said, her eyes on Dannon.

"What about your relief?" Dannon asked, his teasing smile dragging a roll of Flora's sky-blue eyes.

"I'll send Moore in three hours. If I haven't heard from you before then, I'll send the fucking entire squad," the woman said. It was obvious she'd meant for Dannon to hear it.

Three hours. That was more than enough time to tie Flora to Dannon. Wait. No. That's not what he wanted. He just wanted to bury his dick in her and get her the fuck out of his head. Once he screwed her, he could move on and stop fantasizing about the Succubus staring at him with narrowed eyes.

"Got it. Call you later." Flora ended the call and pushed the door open. Dannon reached down and offered his hand, but Flora ignored it and climbed from the small car, locking it up before turning to follow Dannon. "Well?" she asked, crossing her arms over her breasts. But not quick enough. He'd seen how her nipples puckered through her thin bra and strained against the fabric of her tank top.

"Would you like a formal tour?" he asked with a chuckle, grabbing her arm and wrapping it through the crook of his elbow.

"Why does it seem like you're trying to seduce me?" she asked, tugging at her arm half-heartedly, but Dannon wouldn't release his hold. She could very well pull away if she wanted; she was as strong as he was and just as fast. She wanted his touch. He could smell her lust rolling from her in waves.

Dannon took her through the garage door, holding it open for her to step through. He waited for her reaction as she stood in the open floor plan and turned in a slow circle.

"Not what I expected," she admitted.

Why did her opinion suddenly matter so much? He looked around his space and tried to see it how she did. A long, dark brown couch, a couple of sitting chairs, a big ass, expensive television that took up a quarter of one wall. There were no family photos, but there was art and a lot of it. The walls were painted in neutral, warm tones, and the floor was made of a beautiful oak. He might have been rough around the edges, but he liked his home to be warm. It reminded him of his childhood when things were far simpler.

"What exactly did you expect?" he asked.

Flora turned and looked up at him. Her lips quirked up at the corners. She shrugged. "Gray walls, dark leather, clutter everywhere. You know…a bachelor pad." She stepped further in to the room and ran a hand over the back of the couch, her fingers just barely grazing the top. "What about the rest of the house?"

He nodded and waved a hand ahead of him. She walked down a short hallway and hesitated. He opened the first door, which was a bedroom he'd turned into his office. Again, warm, neutral colors dominated. The bathroom was updated but still simple with a shower on the far wall, a pedestal sink, and tile walls and floor.

The last door on the right was where he stopped her. "This is just my bedroom," he said, stepping in front of her as she reached for the knob.

"Something in there you don't want me to see?" she asked, cocking one dark brow at him.

Ha. There was a lot he wanted her to see in there, but, hell, he'd let her see it anywhere in his house. With a shrug, he turned the knob and pushed the door open, letting her step in ahead of him.

Sliding his hand along the wall, he flipped on the light, filling it with the dim, warm bulb he'd installed. Three walls were painted a rich tan, almost brown. The fourth wall, the one his bed butted up against, was painted a deep, blood red. This was his favorite room. This was more of who he was as an Incubus—the sensual colors, the rich, soft fabrics, the way the room just screamed sex was what he was as a species.

When Flora turned to look in to his eyes, he knew she felt it. Without waiting for her to make the move, Dannon wrapped a hand around the back of her neck and lowered his head, claiming her lips. And that was exactly what he was doing; he was claiming her, making her his, if only for tonight.

A helpless, sexy moan escaped from her lips. But just like at the club, she didn't fight hard or for long. Her hands blazed a trail up his chest to his neck where she clung to him, pulling him closer, pressing her soft body against his. Whether it was because of their natural libido, the sexual tension, or the fact she was hot as fuck and finally in his bedroom, Dannon didn't know, nor did he care to decipher it, but he was close to losing control.

With one hand tangled in Flora's shoulder length blonde hair, he let his other hand roam down her back to her soft, round ass. Damn. She had a body made for touching. Her hands left his neck to caress his face, his chest, then moved south to undo his pants.

Holy shit. This was going to happen. The second her warm hand circled his cock, he moaned in to her mouth, his hips twitching forward of their own accord. He couldn't remember the last time his body reacted like that to a woman. Then again, he hadn't crushed on a woman in years. He wanted someone, he got her. It wasn't often that he was turned down; something about the draw of his kind.

Pulling his mouth from hers, Dannon reached down and yanked her shirt over her head, his hands going immediately to cup

18

her firm tits. They weren't big, but they were the perfect size for his hands and his mouth. Yanking the cups down, he dipped his head and sucked first one then the other nipple in to his mouth. She arched her back, her hands tangling in his short hair and holding him there as if she needed more.

He'd give her as much as she needed as long as he got to feel her wrapped around him before his three hours were up.

Like a damn teenager, Dannon's hands trembled as he struggled to unbutton and unzip her tight jeans. He slipped his hand under her panties and cupped her sex as he continued to lick and suck on her nipples. Fuck. She was so warm. So wet and ready for him. His finger slid in to her with ease and her pussy throbbed once around his finger.

And there went the last of his control. He'd fantasized about taking his time with her, tasting every inch of her until she was begging him to fuck her. Instead, he was about to come just from her soft fingers gliding slowly up and down his shaft.

Turning her and walking her backward, he followed her down when she toppled back on to the mattress. He tugged at her jeans, pulling them down her legs and tossing them to the floor. She helped him lower his pants down his ass but pulled him to her before he could remove them fully. Anxious little thing. He knew the feeling.

Pushing her knees back, he settled between her legs and pushed in to her hard and fast, pulling a scream from those sexy ass lips. He'd imagined her wrapping those lips around his dick, her eyes turned up to him as she sucked him off. But he couldn't wait. Not now. Now, he needed to drill her until they both came.

And from the tingling starting in his balls, he knew he couldn't hold out long. She was so fucking tight, so warm and wet, and the sounds coming from her mouth just urged him on faster, harder until his balls tightened and there was no more holding back.

Throwing his head back, he yelled out his release as every muscle in his body tightened and pressure built, his cock throbbing with each spurt. He'd meant to pull out. He'd meant to cum on her stomach. But now he was filling her with wave after wave of his hot seed.

After a few seconds, that all-encompassing sensation passed and he was mortified—he'd come before her. He'd been so lost in the sensation of her pussy gripping his dick that he'd allowed himself to go before her.

Holy fuck. Never, not once had he finished before making sure the woman he was banging got off at least once.

And as she stared up at him, he realized he'd fucked up.

Chapter Two

Here she was, looking up in to Dannon's eyes after he'd blown his load. Before her. And inside of her. Lucky for that mother fucker she couldn't get knocked up by another of her kind. Only humans could impregnate a Succubus. Same for Incubi. A curse and a gift.

As Dannon stared down at her wide-eyed, he seemed embarrassed and shocked. Why was he shocked? Did he not think he'd get off with her? Or was he shocked that he'd come before her? Did he really think she'd come that quickly or that easily? Hell. They'd barely had any foreplay before he'd plunged in to her.

His dick was awesome; nice and thick and long. But she'd only gotten to feel him deep inside of her for all of five minutes before he blew. As Dannon pulled from her, his eyes still wide, he quickly yanked his pants up, tucking his softening dick away.

"Well. That was fun," she said, pushing up to her elbows. She could feel his jizz sliding down the crack of her ass as she held her thighs tightly shut. "Could you get me a towel or something?"

His head wagged side to side. "I'm sorry," he said. "That's never... You're just so fucking tight... Fuck." He pushed his hand through his long hair and kept shaking his head.

Stepping in to an adjoining bathroom across from the bed, he reemerged with a towel. Pushing her thighs apart, he cleaned her, his head still moving side to side like he was in shock or something. Whatever. So he blew his wad too soon. That happened sometimes.

But now she was frustrated and growing rapidly irritable. In the week she'd been watching him, she'd built this image of the sexy biker. She'd pictured him being some kind of sex guru. An orgasm expert. Nope. Just another guy who couldn't hold back.

Maybe that was a compliment to her that men tended to go so quickly. But that still left her with too much pressure low in her belly. She officially had the female version of blue balls. Yanking the towel from his hand, Flora sat up and finished cleaning herself, then stood to grab her jeans.

"No. This isn't right," Dannon said, watching her bend to pull her jeans over her legs.

"What?" she asked, not bothering to look at him.

Before she could get her other foot in to the leg hole of her worn-in jeans, she was tossed back on to the bed, bouncing lightly only once before her knees were pushed apart. She opened her mouth to protest, to tell him not to bother, but his tongue against her clit stopped any coherent thoughts she might have had.

So fucking sexy. Even with some of him still in her pussy, he was licking her, sucking her clit between his lips. Then he slipped a finger in to her pussy, slowly pumping in to her. Wet sounds filled the room, mixing with her moaning, her mewling, her heavy breathing. Talented tongue. Wicked fingers. Just as she'd thought, those digits were perfect for finger fucking. He slid a second in to her, his tongue working her in quick motions, flicking her clit.

She was so close. Pressure. So much fucking pressure was building. If he stopped before she finished, she might just kill him and make it look like self-defense. "Yes," she breathed out. "Almost there."

His moans increased and the vibration was like one of her toys she kept hidden under her mattress. And then she was tumbling. Little explosions lit up behind her eyes as her hips raised with an intense orgasm. Fuck. Yes. That was what she'd imagined when she'd fantasize about him at night when she worked herself to a frenzy with her favorite battery-operated friend.

His tongue slowed, his fingers pulled from her, and he sucked lightly on her clit as the aftershocks began to fade. As he rose to his knees, he swiped the back of his hand across his mouth, wiping her from his chin and lips. And she had the urge to pull him down for a kiss so she could taste herself on him.

"That's better," he said, a satisfied glint in his eyes.

"That doesn't let you off the hook, quick draw," she said, accepting her shirt as he picked it up from the floor and handed it to her. Her tits still played peek-a-boo so she pulled the cups of her bra back over them and pulled her shirt on.

Dannon slid her panties up her legs and over her hips when she raised her ass. He was dressing her. Was he in a hurry to get her out of his house now that he'd gotten what he'd wanted? Was this his motive when he'd invited her there?

Who was she kidding? This was the exact reason she'd accepted the invite. She'd hoped he'd fuck her. Hell. Chief Jarbo gave her three hours instead of the original one because she was the same as Flora and probably knew she'd end up naked at some point. Flora knew as a fact the Chief had fucked a few witnesses over the time she'd been in the precinct. She'd probably fucked half the damn force, as well.

"You hungry?" Dannon asked, surprising the shit out of her.

Stopping with her pants halfway up her legs, she frowned at him. He watched her expectantly, waiting for her answer. Was he serious? "This isn't a date, Michaels."

"We back to last name status again, Grumio?" he asked.

Well damn. She preferred her real name on his lips. But she couldn't let herself get too attached to him just in case he did end up being the ruthless killer he was suspected of. Honestly, she didn't see it. And if he had killed all those men, they'd deserved it, every last one of them. They were pedophiles, rapists, serial women beaters—the scum of the fucking planet.

"That was fun and all, but it was a onetime deal," she said, zipping up her pants.

"Doubt it," he said.

Opening her mouth to remind him of his quick finish, she snapped it shut. She wouldn't be baited. Not by him. Anyone else could see her anger, see the rage she held in, but not him. She didn't know why, but she felt like it would make her appear weak, vulnerable. And that was a state she refused to allow him to see.

"You still have over two hours before your relief comes," he said, taking a step toward her.

She held out her hand, placing it firmly on his chest. "I'll wait outside."

Why did he suddenly look hurt? The bastard could fuck anyone he wanted; he could convince any woman to drop her panties. So why did he care if she'd just used him for a one-night-stand? Why did he care if she'd used him to sate her need?

And why did she feel a little guilty over how she was making him feel? He was no one to her. Just a sexy as fuck suspect she got the privilege of following around, spending almost every day watching him file one woman after another in to his house?

The thought of him with another woman didn't exactly make her jealous, but for some reason, she hoped she'd left enough of an impression on him he wouldn't want anyone else for a while.

Possessive. That was what she was feeling. A little possessive. And fuck if that didn't just piss her off even more.

"I'll see you," she said, stepping away from him and leaving his house.

The night was closing in and the temperature had dropped a little, bringing chills to her arms. She'd dressed for the hot summer temps and hadn't thought about the fact she'd be sitting in her cool car once the sun dropped. The humidity was remarkably low for St. Louis that time of year. As much as she hated what that did to her hair, at least it would've kept the air a little warmer.

Pulling her phone from her back pocket as she opened her car door, she hit the Chief's number. She answered, but Flora heard moaning in the background. Was she fucking or watching? Flora's need rose again, but she tamped it down, picturing the crushed look on Dannon's face as she'd left him standing alone in his bedroom.

"Yeah?" Jane answered.

"Nothing out of the ordinary in his home."

"You inspected all of it?"

Flora was silent a moment. Actually, no. She had no idea if the home had a basement or not, and hadn't bothered checking out Dannon's office. She'd pretty much stopped the moment she'd stepped in to his erotic bedroom.

"You fucked him, didn't you?" Jane said, amusement in her tone.

"Yep."

24

"Was he good?"

Flora chewed on the inside of her cheek and glanced up at the house in time to see the curtain drop back in place. Had he been watching her? Or was he just making sure she was still out there? "Yeah. He was good." And fast. But she left that part out. Maybe he'd just been too turned on. Or maybe she was just that sexy. Yeah; she'd stick with that excuse. It made her feel a little better about the whole thing.

"I'll send Moore now. Go home. Get some rest. Back on at ten hundred." Another moan hit Flora's ear just before her boss ended the call. She briefly wondered who the Jane was with, but quickly pushed it from her mind. She probably didn't want to know.

Leaning her seat back a little, Flora rested her head against the seat and turned the radio on, keeping the sound low. Headlights flashed across her face as a car came down the street, passing Dannon's house a little too slowly. Turning her upper body, she watched as the car stopped and sat in the middle of the road for a few seconds, the taillights bright in the dark night, and then took off with a rush of the engine. That couldn't have been coincidental.

Had they seen Flora sitting in her car? Did they know who she was? If anyone had been checking Dannon out lately, they had to know he was constantly under police surveillance.

Pushing the door open, Flora tucked her Glock in the back of her pants and crossed the street, moving to stand in the shadows near his garage. She'd wait there until her replacement showed up. Then he could take up guard duty.

No one was going to sneak up on her man; not on her watch.

Shit. No. She'd meant her suspect. Fuck.

Moore had spelled her less than an hour later. That car hadn't come back, but Flora couldn't get the strange fear for Dannon's safety out of her mind. Why? Why was she afraid for him? He could obviously take care of himself and he'd surrounded himself with some of the baddest and scariest mother fuckers she'd ever seen. One call and his little army would rush to his aid.

So why, then, did she have the urge to tell Moore to go home so she could make sure Dannon was safe?

Rolling on to her stomach, she tucked the pillow tightly under her head. He might have come quickly, but his dick had stretched her almost to the point of discomfort. Had he held out for another five minutes, she would've come around him.

His beard had tickled and scratched against the lips of her pussy, against her thighs as he'd worked his head side to side, as he'd licked and sucked her. She'd never been eaten by a man with a beard; fuck, she'd been missing out. That extra sensation aided in sending her over the edge.

Sliding her hand between her body and the mattress, she dipped it between her panties and touched her lips, slipping between until she touched her clit. Swollen again at just the memory of being with Dannon. She'd told him it was a onetime thing, but if she were to be honest, she wanted more. She wanted him to fill every hole. She wanted to see how far he would go with her. How far he could take her. How far she could push him.

Flora pushed a finger in to her hole and pretended it was Dannon's. His fingers were long and nimble and, when he'd turned them and bent them up, he'd rubbed her g-spot with just enough pressure to drive her crazy.

Fucking her own hand, Flora fantasized about his face buried between her legs again. She imagined dropping to her knees in front of him and taking that thick cock in to her mouth, lapping at the drop of pre-cum at the engorged head. She pictured him bending her over that brown couch and yanking her pants to her ankles, positioning himself behind her, and pounding in to her hard enough to rock the couch.

With a soft moan, she came on her own hand, the pulsing walls squeezing her fingers as she slowed the pumping and tapped her clit a couple times to prolong the waves of aftershocks.

Dannon was going to turn out to be a very dangerous man, but not to society. He would end up being dangerous to her body, mind, and heart if she let him.

Chapter Three

Flora dressed in a groggy haze. She hadn't slept well after her little self-indulgence. Images of Dannon doing the same, pulling on his dick as he thought about her, plagued her dreams. Then there were nightmares of a car full of faceless men crashing in to his house and slitting his throat while he slept.

"Shit," she muttered, pulling her shoes on as she sat on the edge of the bed. Her shower had been quick, she'd brushed her teeth almost too vigorously, and had pulled the brush through her hair hard enough to yank a few strands out. She was crabby.

The car ride to her local Starbucks was silent; even the music coming from her cheap speakers irritated her. It was almost as if she were going through withdrawals. Dannon withdrawals. She snorted at that. No way could she be addicted to him after one short tryst.

Iced mocha in hand, Flora used one hand to steer through the streets of West St. Louis County, grumbling at the perfectly manicured yards as if it were their fault for her current mood. She liked her house in the woods. She liked that she had no neighbors. She liked the fact she could have as many men over to bang as she wanted and no one could judge her.

Moore was parked along the front of Dannon's house, the rear of his Mustang facing her as she neared him. When she pulled alongside, she shook her head. The asshole had his head back and was fast asleep, mouth hanging open with a thin line of drool rolling down his chin.

Laying her hand on her steering wheel, she held the horn in place and laughed as Moore jerked up, his head swiveling side to side like he didn't know where he was. As he gained his wits and realized it was Flora who'd woken him, he flipped her the bird then rolled down his window.

"Thanks, asshole."

"How can you watch him with closed eyes?" she teased. She actually liked Joe Moore. He was cocky and young, but he was good at his job and gave great head. And was her closest friend.

"I was just resting my eyes," he said, using the back of his wrist to wipe the drool from his chin.

"You're off. Go home," she said, glancing up at the house. Luckily for Joe, the garage door was open and Dannon's bike was still parked where he'd left it.

Wait. Why hadn't he closed the door after Flora had left? "Did anyone come by last night? Dark sedan, tinted windows?"

Joe frowned and looked off to the side. With a shake of his head, he said, "Not between the time you left and six this morning."

"I take it that's when you decided to rest your eyes?" The asshole had been asleep for at least three or more hours. She nodded at Dannon's garage. "Did he ever close the garage?"

"Nope. He turned off the light around three, though."

He'd left the porch light on all that time? Why? "Report in to the Chief. I'll see you later."

He smiled at her, his eyes swollen from sleep. "How about you climb in and help with this morning wood?"

Flora couldn't help herself; she smiled back. "Sorry, chump. You'll have to rub one off when you get home."

"You're no fun," he teased, waving as he rolled up his window and started his older Mustang. Yep, Joe gave great head, but blew his load with no warning when she gave him head. She didn't mind a little jizz in her mouth every once in a while, but some warning was always nice.

Waiting until Joe's car disappeared around the corner, Flora pushed the door open and strode across the street. After her nightmares, she was a little worried. Why wouldn't he lock up a motorcycle that looked as expensive as this one? Trying the garage door, she straightened when it turned. He hadn't locked it ... or someone had broken in.

Pulling her phone from her pocket and gripping her gun in her other hand, Flora prepared to call in backup if she found anything out of the ordinary.

29

"Dannon?" she called out.

No answer. Moving further in to the house, she quickly peeked around the corner then headed down the hallway. "Dannon." Still no answer.

Flora checked first the office on the right and then glanced in to the dark and empty bathroom before heading toward his closed bedroom door. Taking a deep breath, she turned the knob and pushed it open.

Dannon lie on his back, his arm thrown over his head, his breathing deep and steady. The fucker was asleep. How had he not heard her calling out to him? What if she'd been the enemy or someone out to kill him? Hell. What if she'd just been some low life thief out to steal his precious bike?

Moving closer to the bed and reaching a hand forward to shake him awake, she stilled at the tent his hard cock was creating out of the sheet. Fuck. Even in his sleep that thing was always ready. Tempted to pull the sheet back to touch the silky skin of his shaft, she turned her attention back to his face. He was looking right at her.

"I waited for you," he said, his voice thick with sleep.

"What? Are you talking in your sleep?"

Moving too fast for her to react, Dannon wrapped a hand around Flora's wrist and pulled her to the bed. He rolled on top of her. "I left the door unlocked in case you decided you wanted to come back." He glanced at the window where the sun peeked through the crack. "Took you long enough."

Okay. This was where she told him to get off her, told him she was on duty, that she was working. Instead, she opened her legs to make room for his big body. His hard, long dick pressed against her core through her jeans and he rocked his hips, rubbing her even through the rough material.

This time, he didn't kiss her. He dipped his head and kissed a line between her tank top clad breasts, lifting the bottom hem to nip and lick her belly, working his way up. With her shirt up around her neck, he pulled one cup of her bra down, releasing her tit, and lapped at the tightening bud. So unprofessional. She should get up.

No. He should go down.

Moaning, her hips pushed up to meet his, begging for more of that delicious friction he was causing with each circle of his pelvis. "Beg me," he breathed against her nipple. Hot and cold. Shaking her head, she refused. No. He needed to beg her. She was the dominant one.

Right?

As his hand lowered to cup her pussy through her jeans, she tried to remember who was in charge. His palm pressed hard against her, right over her clit, and she cried out.

"Beg me," he said, his voice deep and gravelly.

"No," she moaned out. Damn it. She'd meant for that to come out as a true protest.

Lowering down her body, Dannon unbuttoned her pants, then ripped her zipper down. Peeling them down her legs, his beard scraped against her tender flesh, raising gooseflesh across her exposed arms and legs.

Raising back up her body, he claimed her lips in a toe curling, body melting kiss as his hand slid in to her panties, through her folds, and expertly found her clit. This was what she'd imagined every time she'd fantasized about him taking her. This heart pounding, breath racing, body trembling foreplay. Hell. If he kept this up, she'd come before he even entered her.

"I'm going to fuck you with my hand until you come all over my fingers. And then you're going to beg me for my big dick. Do you hear me?"

She nodded. She couldn't force her voice out as he plunged his finger in to her roughly, working it deep, slow, adding another. Two fingers. Holy shit. Three fingers. And now she was stretched as he worked her, finger fucked her wet pussy, the sounds filling the room. Pressure. Pressure. So much pressure.

Adding his thumb to the equation and rubbing her clit with the thick pad, he fingered her hard and fast, his palm slapping against her with each pump. And then she cried out his name as her pussy clenched his fingers with each wave.

"Good girl. Come all over my fingers." He kept pumping in to her, drawing each wave from her until the pressure built again. He

31

was pulling another orgasm from her. "Now, beg me. Beg me for my dick. Beg me to fuck you."

"Please, fuck me. Fuck me hard. Make me come," she cried out, her head rocking side to side as the sensation became almost too much to bear.

Pulling his fingers from her and using her own come to slick his dick, he gripped the base in his big hand, positioned it over her hole, then slid in to her in one thrust, stretching her even further. "Yes. Fuck me. Please. Fuck me hard," she begged.

Gripping her wrists in his hands, he held them over her head and rocked his hips, his pelvic bone rubbing her clit, his balls slapping against her as he gave it to her hard, as he fucked her fast, as the bed rocked and hit the wall with each thrust.

"When you come, I want to hear my name on those pretty lips again," he demanded.

She was dominant. She was…oh, fuck it. For once, it was nice to submit to someone. Especially Dannon as he filled her pussy and dragged another body rocking orgasm from her.

"Oh fuck. I'm coming. Yes, Dannon. I'm coming again," she cried out, her eyes squeezed shut, her back bowing with the explosion. Her stomach tightened, her hips raised, and her heart stuttered. It was so intense it was almost painful. And now she was hooked. If he could do this to her body, she knew it would be damn near impossible to turn her back on him again.

As he kept pumping in to her even as her pulsing pussy calmed, she realized he'd been carried away last night, just as she had. He'd probably built that moment in his head for the week they'd been watching each other, wondering about each other, fantasizing about what the other would be like in bed.

This time, he lasted thirty minutes before throwing his head back and barking out his release, her name on his lips this time. With trembling arms, he dropped his weight on to her, holding the bulk on his elbows, and rested his face in her neck. His warm breath washed across her chest as his heart thundered against her.

"Good morning," he said after a few silent minutes.

32

Tapping his side, she shoved at him to get his body off her. She was burning up now. Rolling to his side, Dannon rested his head on his elbow. "That's how I wanted the first time to go," he admitted, pushing a hand through his messy hair.

"So you planned this? You planned on making me scream your name," she said with a teasing smile.

"Oh. I plan all kinds of things for that tight body. That tight ass, too," he said, reaching over and squeezing one of her tits.

And now she was picturing him drilling in to her ass and was getting hot all over again. Maybe that was his thing; maybe he was an ass man. She'd been with lots of guys who preferred to come on or in her ass. Not her number one favorite thing, but not exactly her least, either.

"You my escort today?" he asked. She frowned at him. Why did that almost sound dirty?

"Yes. I'm your surveillance today," she said, pushing up to lean against the headboard. She tucked her tit back in to her bra and pulled her shirt down. "You need to close your garage door at night," she admonished.

He frowned at her with a smile. "Aw. Were you worried about me?" She snorted. "If I'd locked it, how would you have gotten in this morning?"

"I only came in because it was open and I was worried our suspect had been murdered."

His face went serious, any hint of amusement gone. "Your suspect," he repeated.

"Well, yeah. You're not exactly my boyfriend. I'm a cop. I'm here because of the missing sickos...I mean, missing men."

"The first one was correct," he said, throwing his legs over the side and rolling his head on his shoulders. "And I know nothing about them."

"I don't care if you do or not," she admitted. She didn't want him to confess to her because she'd be required to turn him in. She wasn't about to go to prison for him. But, she wasn't exactly sad those sons of bitches were gone. "I'm just doing my job. I don't give two shits if they're ever found. And don't say another word to me about

33

it," she said, throwing up her hand to stop him when he looked over his shoulder and opened his mouth.

"That other guy from last night … Moore? He your boyfriend?" he asked, his tone and eyes strictly curious.

"Nah. Just a fuck buddy."

Turning and leaning on a locked arm, he smiled. "Is that what I am?"

"I think we'd have to screw around more than twice to be categorized as fuck buddies."

"Challenge accepted," he said, standing and presenting a beautifully toned and tanned ass. He pulled a pair of jeans from the top of his dresser and yanked them up his legs, jumping a little as he tucked his semi-wood in to his pants. "I swear I'm always hard around you," he said, shimmying strangely to zip up his pants without catching the skin of his pecker in the zipper.

"I'll be outside," she said, shaking her head with a chuckle. Unlike last night, he didn't appear hurt or disappointed. He just nodded and pulled a shirt over his head.

An hour later, Dannon emerged, something wrapped in a napkin in his hand, his long hair damp, and his smile bright. Shit. Dangerous! "I brought you some breakfast. Long day today."

"It's technically lunch time," she said, taking the bagel from his hand. "Thanks." She smiled up at him as he nodded his head. "Why is it a long day?"

"Lots of errands. Unless, of course, you want the day off?"

"Ha! Yeah. That would be great. Maybe you could just call my boss and request one for me."

"Just say the word," he teased, walking backward.

Turning, he strode toward his motorcycle, his ass hot in those holy jeans, his strides long and confident, and then threw one leg over the machine. Twisting a rubber band around his hair, he pulled on a black skull cap and started his bike. It rumbled to life and Flora could swear her pussy woke up at the sound. Damn him and his panty soaking ways.

Walking it backward out of the garage, he nodded at Flora once, then took off out of the neighborhood. A day off. Yeah; that would be great. She'd love a day to herself. A day to refill her energy with as much lust as she could. Her kind did best with constant fucking. No. That wasn't completely true; she could get her fill by feeding off others' lust just as quickly, but how much fun was that?

Like now. Now, she was full of energy from her thorough fucking Dannon had given her. This would hold her over for hours. And it was a hell of a lot more fun than sitting in the strip joint and filling up on the lust pouring from a bunch of college boys or horny perverts.

She'd actually begged Dannon to fuck her. She'd begged him for his dick. She'd never done that before, actually submitted to a man's demands. And she liked it. A lot. She didn't know if she'd admit that to him or anyone else, but she really wanted him to boss her around more in the bedroom, tell her what to do, tell her what he wanted.

Shifting in her seat and rubbing her thighs together to cause a little friction between her legs, Flora shook her head as Dannon pulled in to the post office. "Oh, come on," she grumbled, resting her elbow on the door and holding her head in her hand. He was right; this was going to be a long fucking day.

Flora sat at her desk and typed out the report on her day with Dannon. Exactly zero things of interest happened. Nope. Not true. But she couldn't put two orgasms in her report. That had nothing to do with the investigation.

Moaning came from Chief Jarbo's office and Flora stuffed an ear bud in to her ear to drown it out. One of the best and worst things about working for the ParaPolice was everyone involved understood there were some species who had to get their willies off more than others. Just like the vamps needed blood, the Fairies, Pixies, and Succubae and Incubi needed sex. It was just part of life for them. Sex didn't equal love. Hell. Half the time, they didn't even like the person they were fucking; it was just a means to an end.

Flora clicked on Dannon's mug shot and stared at it. There were three different photos of him in different years. But in each of them, he stared in to the camera with those intense brown eyes as if he was staring in to the soul of the photographer. His hair was longer in the most recent one and he'd grown a beard recently, but otherwise, he hadn't changed much. Once their kind reached puberty, they stopped aging.

A hand landed on Flora's shoulder and she jumped with a yelp. She yanked the ear buds out and silenced the sounds of heavy bass from her favorite Korn song. "Holy shit, Joe. You scared the crap out of me."

"Sorry. I said your name."

"Yeah, well, I was trying to block out Jane and her date."

"We're done now," Joe said.

Flora did a double take and stared up in to Joe's eyes. "That was you in there?" Joe was a Pixie, which was why she was one of his favorite friends with benefits; he could go over and over again until Flora was sated.

But she'd had no idea he was banging their boss, too. Was she the only one in the office who'd yet to play with Jane's pussy?

"Yeah. I was bargaining for a day off. You should try it."

"If I have to fuck my boss for a day off, I'll just keep working."

"I forgot; strictly dick," Joe said, mimicking her. "She had a strap on," he offered. Turning to glare up at Joe, she shook her head as he held up his hands and backed away. "I'm joking. You off?"

"Almost. A few more things to wrap up."

"Like staring at Dreamy Dannon," he said, grasping his hands under his chin and batting his eyes.

"Whatever. You'd do him."

"Fuck yeah, I would. Look at him," Joe said, leaning forward to get a better look at his picture. "But, he's strictly pussy." Poor thing sounded dejected. All Pixie were bisexual, while her kind and the Fae could be straight, gay, or bi. Sometimes it seemed life would be easier if she enjoyed both.

"Go home, Joe," she said, pushing him away from her computer.

"I'll wait for you." Those four words were loaded. He'd just gotten off with the Chief, but Flora and he had chemistry in the bedroom and he knew how to play her like a fucking upright bass.

Thirty minutes later, Flora was bent over her couch with Joe's fingers digging in to her hips. His dick wasn't as long or thick as Dannon's, but she still liked. He knew how to work her, where to touch her, how hard to fuck her.

When she moaned out with her release, she realized it was nothing like her orgasm with Dannon. Joe finished her, but it wasn't mind blowing and her legs didn't feel like jelly. A few more thrusts and Joe pulled from her, finishing on her ass cheeks. She stayed leaned over the couch, holding her weight on her forearms while Joe retrieved a towel from her bathroom and cleaned her. His touch wasn't gentle like Dannon's had been; the gesture wasn't erotic. It was just another session with her buddy.

Joe pecked her on the cheek once they were dressed and Flora walked him to the door. As he pulled it open, she started hard when she found Dannon standing on the other side, his hand raised to knock.

"What are you doing here? How do even know where I live?"

"Hey, Dannon," Joe said, his eyes making a sweep of Dannon's tall, muscular body.

"Hey, Moore," Dannon said, his eyes glued to Flora.

Leaning around him and peering outside, she growled. "Where's your tail?"

"I lost them."

"You what?" she shrieked, stomping in to the living room to grab her phone.

"You really want them to know I'm here?"

Pausing with her phone in her hand, she glanced at Joe, who was shaking his head behind Dannon. "Fuck," she growled out, tucking it in to her back pocket. "Bye, Joe," she said, waving at Joe as he stepped through the door.

37

Joe smiled big, shot her a thumbs up, and glanced at Dannon once before pulling the door shut.

"How do you know where I live?"

"You're not the only one who knows how to follow people around," he said, stalking toward her. She retreated, matching him step by step.

"You had your buddies follow me?"

"Feels shitty, doesn't it?" he said, still stalking toward her, his eyes roaming from her braless chest to her unbuttoned pants. She hadn't bothered to fully dress because she planned to shower as soon as Joe left.

"It's my job," she said, her voice coming out far breathier than she'd intended. This was the passion she'd missed when she'd let Joe screw her. Her body didn't tighten, her pussy didn't grow wet just from the sight of Joe. But with Dannon? Her body was primed and ready for him. His eyes on her felt like fingers strumming her every nerve.

"Where's your bathroom?" he asked, stalking until her back hit the wall and she could go no further.

She jerked her head toward a hallway to the left. Moving in a blur, he grabbed her and threw her over his shoulder, carrying her down the hall, his shoulder hard against her stomach. "What the fuck are you doing?" she asked. This wasn't exactly where she'd thought they were going with their little cat and mouse game they'd been playing in the living room.

Dropping her to her feet and causing the room to spin as the blood rushed back to her head, he ripped the lavender shower curtain to the side and turned on the water. "Dannon. What are you doing?"

His eyes were lighter now, almost gold as his essence pushed forward. They weren't exactly animals, but they were far from humans. The demon that resided within them could rip through his façade at any point and take the lead.

His hands rough, he tore her tank top down the center then reached for her pants. "Don't you dare rip these. They're my favorite," she said, shoving his hands away and pushing her pants down to her ankles.

38

She stepped out of them. Dannon was naked in a blur, and she squeaked as he picked her up and stepped in to the shower with her in his arms. The water beat against her, steam filling the bathroom as Dannon lowered her slowly, his hard cock rubbing against her side.

"Turn around," he ordered, his voice too gravelly to pass as human. Oooh. She really liked him like this. He was losing control over his humanoid façade and she'd caused it. She wondered if any of his other lays had ever seen his true form before? She was tempted to drop her shield and revel in letting him see her wholly, but wanted to see his first.

Letting him turn her with rough hands on her shoulders, she lifted her head and let the water beat down her naked chest. The rough texture of a terry cloth washcloth started at the top of her spine and moved down her ass. He scrubbed her gently, making little circles over every inch of her back and ass before moving down her legs. "Face me," he barked out. She turned and he moved from her feet up, hesitating on her pussy before moving to her throat.

Why was he bathing her? Why was he so primal right now? What was causing him to lose control of his shield?

When she looked up in to his blazing eyes, she smiled as he opened his mouth to reveal four pointy fangs poking through his gums. A little more. Just a little more. But she had no idea what was causing this so she didn't know how to push him further.

"His scent was all over you," he said, his fingers softer now as they grazed down her arms to her ribs. He caressed the flesh on her sides, barely brushing the sides of her boobs.

So that was what this was about; Joe had marked her with his scent when he'd come on her ass. But Flora had planned on washing it off, anyway. She had no idea Dannon was on his way to her house when Joe was slipping her his willy.

Intent on seeing all of him, on watching him drop his façade and reveal his true form, she decided it was time to push all of his buttons. "He always marks me after he fucks me," she said, turning and bending to turn off the water. Stepping over the side of the tub, she glanced at him over her shoulder. "They all do. Why? Does that bother you?" She turned to face him as water droplets rolled down her body. "Does it bother you to think about Joe's dick pumping inside of me? Does it bother you to think of other men shooting their cum on me, on my tits, my ass, my stomach?"

She turned to saunter from the room, putting just the right amount of sway in to her bare ass when a loud roar made her smile. Holy shit. She'd done it. Rounding the corner in to her bedroom, she waited for him to join her. She'd known him for just over a week, had only fucked him twice, but he was hers. Shit. She was his. This whole thing might not last past tonight, but she knew no one else would ever affect her the way her sexy Incubus did.

Dannon's steps were heavy as he walked slowly to her room. And there he was. His cheekbones were chiseled and sharp, his lips parted to reveal those fangs she knew would bring her the ultimate pleasure, dark wings sprouted from his back as he rolled his shoulders, and now there was a glow behind the gold of his eyes.

Tossing her head back, she focused on her façade and let it drop. Her eyes, like his, would be glowing, but hers glowed white. Her wings were smaller than his and a dark gray tipped with white at the ends. But her cheekbones were as sharp as his, her fangs pointy and slightly smaller. This was who they were. What they were. And tonight, in her bedroom, they would feed from each other as nature intended.

Dannon stalked toward her, but this time she didn't back away. One hand grabbed her by the nape of her neck while the other wrapped around her back. He pulled her to him, his lips crashing on to hers, his fangs jabbing the tender flesh there. Their tongues dueled as his hard cock stayed trapped between then, pressing against her stomach.

He pulled his mouth from hers. "Turn around," he said, repeating what he'd demanded in the bathroom. Turning, she put her hands on the bed and spread her legs. His finger dipped low, moving from her clit to her puckered asshole. "No one else marks you," he growled out.

"Yes," she agreed. Spread for him like this, knowing what he was about to give her, she'd agree to just about anything if it meant he'd push that cock in to her.

40

"No one," he said, his finger dipping in to her wet pussy. He pumped in to her, slowly, quickly, slowly. It was agonizing. His other hand pushed at the small of her back, making her arch it more, presenting her to him. As he fingered her pussy, he circled a finger of his other hand around her ass. Oh fuck yes. The finger left her, dipped in to her pussy, then returned to slowly breach the tight walls. He'd used the wetness from her pussy as a lube. That alone almost made her come. "I'm going to mark you so all other men know you're off limits. Do you hear me? From here out, you'll only fuck others if I'm there."

"What about you?" she said, shoving back to push his fingers deeper.

"Do you want to see me fuck?"

"If I'm yours, you're mine."

He growled long and low, his fingers working her holes in unison. More. She needed more. She needed her clit stimulated. Removing his fingers from her pussy, he gripped her hip with his free hand and slammed his dick in to her hard. She cried out, throwing her head back at the painful pleasure. He continued to finger fuck her asshole as he drove into her hard, harder.

She was almost there. Almost there. "Yes."

"Say my name, Flora. Who's making you come? Say my fucking name."

"Dannon. Oh, fuck yes, Dannon. I'm coming on your dick." He pulled his finger from her ass and pumped in to her hard and fast, drawing every last quiver from her pussy.

When she stopped pulsing around him, he bent over her, his chest to her back, his mouth near her ear. "You're mine," he said, lifting from her, pulling from her pussy and pressing the hard head against her asshole. "Say it," he said, pushing in to her asshole slowly.

"I'm yours," she breathed out, relaxing to prevent clenching and causing more pain than pleasure.

"Again," he said, pushing further, further, until he was fully sheathed inside her tight ass.

"I'm yours. Dannon, oh fuck, I'm yours," she said as he pulled from her and slowly pushed back in.

"Do you like my dick in your ass?" he growled out.

"Yes. I love it. Please, fuck my ass," she begged. Who the hell was she? What had Dannon done to her? Whatever it was, it felt fucking awesome. It felt normal. It felt natural.

"That's right, Flora. Beg me." He pushed in to her faster, stretching her ass, creating a slight pinch. "Touch yourself," he ordered.

Balancing on one hand, she reached between her legs and pinched her clit between two fingers; it was so swollen she could almost jack it off. Pinching it a few more times, she stroked it, tapped it, slipped a finger inside herself. So wet. So fucking wet.

"I want to feel you come while I'm deep in your ass," he said, his pumps becoming faster, harder.

Rubbing herself faster, she moaned as the pressure built. Reaching back, Flora cupped Dannon's balls; they were tight. He was close, too. Oh hell no. She wanted to come while he was buried inside of her, while he was fucking her ass hard.

Faster, faster, she kept rubbing herself, pushing harder, causing more friction. The orgasm snuck up on her quickly, hardly any buildup as everything tightened then released as she exploded from the inside out.

"Yes. That's right. Squeeze my dick," he said, pounding in to her, stretching her. Ruining her for any other man.

As he barked out his orgasm, he pulled from her and came against her asshole, letting it run down her pussy. With one hand, he rubbed it across her ass cheeks, rubbing it in to her flesh, marking her. And then he bent forward, opened his mouth over the side of her neck, and bit down. His fangs slid in to the delicate flesh there, pulling a scream from Flora's lips. This. This was what she'd wanted. This was who they were. His venom pulled one more flash of pleasure from her before he pulled his fangs slowly from her, lapping his tongue against the wounds to close them.

But there would be a scar now. He'd marked her. He'd bitten her. He'd used his own venom to claim her. Only her kind could cause scars on each other, and he'd done just that. He'd tethered himself to her, marked her as his, carved his name on to her body and in to her heart.

Now that the endorphins were wearing off, she realized the gravity and depth of what she'd just allowed him to do. She would now carry his scent permanently. Any paranormal man she fucked would know who she belonged to.

Mother fucker.

Chapter Four

Flora yanked on a pair of shorts and a tank top, glaring at Dannon the whole time. "What the fuck were you thinking?" she asked.

What the fuck had he been thinking? He'd just come over to mess around. Maybe get his dick wet. He just wanted her to know she was easy for his people to track down. The cop, Joe, was there. No big deal. He knew what she was, knew how much their kind needed. It wasn't jealousy, exactly. But when he'd scented Joe on Flora, when he realized he'd marked her with his scent, something primal, his fucking demon went a little crazy in him. He'd become possessive. And he'd dropped his shield to take her.

But she had, too. And fuck, she was even more beautiful in her true form. Those fucking wings; were they nearly as sensitive as the rest of her? He hadn't even thought to touch them, to stroke them. All he could think about was burying his dick in her, sinking his fangs in to her, and making sure any mother fucker who thought about tapping his woman had to come to him first.

And she hadn't returned the favor.

"I don't know," he lied.

"Bullshit," she said, pulling the collar of her shirt to the side and looking in the mirror to check out the four perfect circles scarring the flesh at the crook of her neck. He hadn't even hidden his bite. He'd made sure it was perfectly visible to any asshole interested in her.

"Fuck. Flora, I don't know. I came here to mess with you. Maybe try to get a little pussy. But when I smelled Joe on you...I don't fucking know. Something in me snapped."

"Yeah. I noticed," she said, shoving past him and stomping from her bedroom.

"Hold on," he said, grabbing her arm and yanking her to a stop. "You knew what you were doing when you started talking about

44

other men coming on you. You were goading me. Baiting me. You wanted to see my beast, and, well, you got it."

"Yeah. I revealed my beast, too, but I didn't fucking mark you," she said, jerking her arm from his grasp.

"Fine. Here. Do it," he said, tilting his head to the side to give her his neck.

"What?"

"Mark me," he said.

"Are you out of your fucking mind? Oh, and by the way, in what universe did you think demanding I only fuck other men when you're around or with your permission was going to fly?"

He stood straight and stared down at her. Fuck. He had said that. What was wrong with him? What was this woman doing to him? Never, literally never in his existence had he cared if a woman carried another man's scent. Never had he cared if the woman he was fucking or even dating still got some on the side. Hell. He did it all the time.

And now, other women suddenly didn't seem to exist.

Glancing down at his naked body, he threw up his hands and left her standing there. He couldn't discuss this shit with his dick flopping around. Grabbing his jeans from her bathroom floor, he pulled them up his legs and tucked his junk away. He didn't bother to zip or button his jeans; he was still too worked up and had zero desire to recreate the scene in Something About Mary.

Flora was on her couch now, her knees pulled up, her arms wrapped around them, her chin resting on top when he returned. How had he not realized just how beautiful she was? He'd thought she was hot as fuck from the second she parked outside his house, but here, with her wings poking through the arm holes of her tank, those perfect sharp cheekbones, her stunning white eyes glowing as she stared at him…his breath caught in his lungs.

Crossing the room slowly, he lowered next to her on the couch. "You can fuck whoever you want," he said, reaching for her. She didn't flinch away, but she didn't nuzzle against his touch, either. "I don't know why I said that."

She kept watching him, her eyes losing a little of their glow. This was the first time he'd been naked in front of a woman. Not in

45

the bodily nude sense, but neither of them bothered to hide themselves, neither of them cast their wings away or covered their essence. "I can't believe you did that," she said, her voice soft. "I can't believe I wanted you to," she muttered, lowering her feet to the floor.

"You wanted me to?" he asked, fighting to keep the triumphant smile from his lips.

"Stop gloating," she said with a roll of her white eyes. If he had his way, this would be how she stayed; this would be how she looked every day. But humans weren't ready for that just yet. And until things changed, they had to work beside the fragile beings on a regular basis.

Scooting closer, he pushed the hair from her face and let his hands lower to her wings. When he closed his forefinger and thumb around the base and stroked it to the end, she shivered. With a smile, she pulled her wings in to her back. "Sorry. They're ticklish," she said. Okay. Not an erogenous zone for her, then.

"I want you to mark me, Flora," he said, his fingertips grazing the sharp edge of her cheekbone. So beautiful. So perfect.

"Why, Dannon? Why would you want that?"

"Because I belong to you. And you belong to me," he said. He thought it was obvious. Then again, he was a little confused by all of this himself. He'd never wanted to be tethered to one woman. He'd never wanted to know everything about someone so badly; wanted to know every inch of her body, know what made her moan, what made her smile. He wanted to buy her an entire fucking library of those mushy books she loved so much.

She kept staring at him, then shook her head. "No."

"No?"

Her head wagged side to side for a few seconds and then she sighed. "Okay, look. If we're going to do this...I can't believe I'm even considering this. You know, I always thought if this shit ever happened, we'd be madly in love. I always thought the person I'd finally let sink his fangs in to me would hold my heart in his hands." What she didn't realize was she was quickly claiming his. How the fuck did that even happen so fast? "If we do this, if I agree to this, there have to be rules," she said, turning to look at him. The glow was completely gone and the white had faded to a pale blue.

"What kinds of rules?" he asked, scooting even closer, the smile stretching across his face.

"Don't get so excited there, demon," she said, holding her hand out to stop his approach. "Number one, you don't own me. You hear me?"

"Yeah. Of course not."

She blew out a huffed breath. "Do you really need to be there if I fuck someone else?"

He glanced away, studied her room. He hadn't even noticed it when she'd opened her door. It was like he had tunnel vision, and all he could focus on was erasing the other man's mark and replacing it with his own. She had an eclectic taste. The walls were painted in robin's egg blue, but nothing matched. There were brightly colored pillows adorning her one long couch, paintings and portraits hung everywhere, there were even letter magnets on her fridge. He narrowed his eyes. Holy shit. She'd spelled out Dannon in primary colored magnets.

Turning his attention back to her with a wide smile, he chuckled when she looked over her shoulder and realized what he'd seen. "Shut up," she mumbled, her cheeks blazing a bright pink. "Answer my question."

Did he? Did he really need to know about everyone she sated her needs with? Yeah. As his beast reared up and threatened to take over, he realized there were two of them in this. And his beast was front and center as he considered all the possibilities. "Compromise," he said, and chuckled when she threw her head back against the couch and groaned. His little she-demon was spunky as hell. "I don't have to be there every time. But at least let me know after. I'm not asking you to shoot me a text every time you're about to get stuffed, but how about after the dude leaves? That way, I'm not surprised when I smell a new guy."

"Or I could just shower after," she said, raising one brow.

"Touché," he said.

"What about you?" she asked.

47

He pictured her in the room as some faceless chick wrapped her lips around his cock, and fuck if his beast didn't roar in his head. "I'd love for you to be there. I think it'd be hot as fuck if you watched."

Her pupils dilated and her eyes lightened to white again. Oh yeah. She liked that idea. "You don't have to tell me every time, though. You're not officially mine," she said, her now glowing eyes dropping to his throat.

"Flora," he said, his voice deep in his own ears.

"What?" she said, her tongue darting out to moisten her lips as she kept staring at the pulse point on his throat.

Dannon leaned closer and tilted his head to the side. And then he did yet something else he'd never done. He begged. "Please. Mark me. Claim me."

As if her own beast took over, Flora launched herself at him, her knees straddling over his lap, and latched on to his throat. Her fangs pricked the skin then sank in. But instead of pulling away immediately, she took three long draws of his blood. Oh, fuck yeah. His dick twitched in his pants, begging to be set free, begging to be buried in Flora's hot pussy again.

But she pulled away, not bothering to close his wounds with her venom, and glared down at him with angry eyes, his blood still on her lips. "And now you're mine, demon," she said, reaching between them to free his cock.

When she pulled her shorts to the side and slid over him, he threw his head back and let her take the reins.

They'd fucked three times since she'd marked him and his beast needed to cover every inch of her. He'd come on her stomach and tits, in her mouth, and in her pussy. He was in her and all over her. After he'd used his hand to rub some of it in, she just wiped the rest away with a towel. She'd never climbed from the bed to shower him off.

Now, she lie asleep beside him. She'd called in to her boss to let them know his tail could just go home; that she'd be responsible for his whereabouts for the rest of the night. He'd covered his mouth to hold back the chuckle as the Chief had regaled her of the fit the other cop threw when he realized Dannon had slipped away while he was busy playing motorboat with one the stripper's big tits.

And here he was, experiencing another of his firsts; he'd never actually slept beside a woman. Maybe he wasn't asleep yet, but he held her with his arms wrapped tightly around her. Even threw one of his legs over hers. What was this feeling? What was going on with him? With his beast? The fucker was practically purring like a cat.

Flora murmured something in her sleep and twitched once. Dannon stroked her hair, calming her in case she was having a nightmare. She relaxed again, sighing his name, and then her breathing became deep and steady again.

Holy shit. She'd said his name in her sleep. Was she dreaming of him? Maybe she was having a sex dream. That was kind of hot.

They'd need to get up soon and he'd yet to sleep. Closing his eyes, he buried his face in her hair and thought about everything that had transpired today. He'd marked Flora Grumio. In their world, that was pretty much the equivalent of getting married. Only there was no divorce, no way to purge them of each other's marks, no way to purge the shared essence from their bodies. They were linked for eternity now, for better or worse.

Oh, they could choose to walk away. They could still fuck other people. But they would never feel the same connection they did with each other. They would never feel the bone deep satisfaction they felt when they were physically connected.

As he thought about her glowing eyes, about the way her tiny fangs felt piercing his skin, he fell asleep wondering if this was what falling in love felt like.

"You're seriously not giving any details," Joe said, leaning against her desk as she scrolled through pictures of some of the missing people Dannon was being accused of killing. She wasn't really paying attention to any of the details. She hadn't been lying or exaggerating when she'd told Dannon she couldn't give two shits if they were ever found.

Fuck. Dannon.

Rolling her head to her shoulder, she stretched the place where Dannon had marked her. Everyone had smelled him on her the second she'd stepped in to the building and their eyes all zeroed in on the two visible scars. If Dannon Michaels went down for murder, she would never be respected by her peers again.

Then again, if Dannon Michaels went down for murder, she'd probably quit her job and become a hermit. The mother fucker was somehow burrowed under her skin and was quickly embedding himself in to her heart. She wasn't sure if she liked this feeling. It made her feel…giddy. Lightheaded and distracted.

"No, Joe. Go away."

"Does this mean we can't fuck anymore?" he asked, hitting a button to turn off her screen.

Turning in her computer chair, she leaned back a little and looked up at her favorite blonde-haired Pixie. "We can still fuck."

"What about Dannon?"

"He'll still fuck others, too."

Joe kept staring at her. "It's so weird that you're fucking mated, man. And to a sex pot like Dannon fucking Michaels. At least tell me this," he said, leaning closer. "Does he have a big dick?"

Smiling up at Joe, she decided to throw him a bone. "Big, long, and thick. And he likes it rough," she said. "He's dominant and demanding as hell, and it makes me hotter than I thought possible."

Joe threw his head back and groaned. "You're killing me."

"You're a slut," she teased, shoving him so she could get back to work.

"Moore, Grumio," Chief Jarbo called out.

They exchanged a look before Flora rolled her chair back from the desk and stood, following Joe in to the Chief's office. "Close the door," she ordered, turning her back on them. When she was behind her desk, she glanced at something below before hiking her skirt up a little and sitting. Flora would bet money there was someone under there waiting for her pussy.

"Since Flora has decided the suspect is her mate, we're going to have to change things up a bit. I assume you no longer want to sit outside his house?" Jane asked Flora. Hell no. She wanted to sit on his face. But instead of saying that out loud, she shook her head. "I figured. Okay. From now on, Flora is lead tail unless she has to leave his side. In that situation, you need to report in so we can get someone else on him."

No one else better be on him. Wait. What the fuck was that? She didn't care who rode his dick, as long as he still belonged to her. "You do know there's nothing to find," Flora said, sitting back and crossing her arms over her chest.

"We've already gone through this. Until I receive other orders, Dannon Michaels is our lead suspect."

"Whatever," Flora grumbled under her breath. She'd been away from him for five hours and already she was getting frustrated. She glanced over at Joe; he was always up for a quick screw in the bathroom stall.

"Flora?" Chief Jarbo barked out.

"What?"

"Are you listening, or are you planning your perfect wedding?"

She snorted. "We're not getting married."

"You kind of already are," Joe said softly, his head down.

"We're not getting married," Flora repeated. "What did you say? I was thinking about..." Come up with a good lie. "I was thinking about who other suspects could be." That sounded forced even in her own head.

"When you find one, let me know." Jane's eyes rolled closed and she breathed heavy. Without opening them, she said, "Dismissed," in a guttural tone. Yep. There was definitely someone under her desk.

When they were back at Flora's desk, Joe looked back at Jane's door. "Who do you think that was?"

Flora opened her mouth to say she didn't care when the Chief's door opened and the receptionist, Caren, sauntered out, adjusting her skirt. Well damn. The Chief really would fuck anyone. "Okay, then," Flora said, dipping her head to avoid Caren's gaze as she passed.

"That's kind of hot," Joe said, watching as Caren headed back up front. "You think they'll let me join next time?"

"Is there anyone you won't fuck?" she teased.

He tapped a finger to his lips, acting like he was actually thinking about it then shook his head. "Nope. Can't think of anyone. I'll see you later. I'm heading out to lunch and then…I don't know. I'm not sure what I'm supposed to be doing now since you're bogarting the suspect."

"Shame he won't mark you, too," she said, sarcasm dripping from every word. "Then you could make sure you're tied to his hip twenty-four/seven."

"I'm having a hard time seeing the bad in that," Joe said as he walked away.

Pulling her phone from her back pocket, Flora pulled Dannon's number up. This would officially be their first text conversation. I'm your new permanent tail.

A few seconds later, her phone dinged. Good. I like fucking your tail.

She smiled like a fool as she typed out, Boo. Bad joke. Where r u? Meet me?

Holding the phone and watching it with anticipation, she warmed all the way through when he sent, Club D. Wear something short and sexy. See you in two hours.

He wanted to meet her at Club Debauchery, which could only mean one thing: It was time to test the waters of their new connection. He'd said he preferred to be there when she fucked but would settle to just be alerted. He, on the other hand, offered to let her watch any time she wanted. And fuck, did she ever. What did that say about her as a person? Shouldn't she want monogamy now that they were kind of married?

She actually laughed out loud to that, then ducked her head when she realized others were staring at her like she'd lost her mind. Monogamy. Her kind wasn't capable of monogamy. Unless they were together every minute of every day, she'd need to find someone else as much as he would. It had already been far too many hours since she'd last fed from Dannon. She could've stayed in the Chief's office and fed from her lust, but she wanted the real thing. Now that she'd tasted the kind of pleasure her connection to Dannon could bring her, she knew she'd never be fully sated by anyone else again.

Chapter Five

Flora approached the line wrapped around the building and groaned. It was going to take forever to get inside, and her mate was waiting. And she couldn't wait much longer to see what he had in store for her tonight.

Pulling her badge from inside her purse, she stepped up to the door man and presented it. "I'm Officer–"

"Flora, yeah. Dannon said you'd be arriving soon. Go on in. He said he'll be at the bar."

Flora frowned slightly but shoved her badge back in her purse. Guess Dannon knew more people than she realized. She pulled at the bottom hem of her dress, checked her cleavage, then sauntered in to the building on her five-inch stilettos. She knew what they did to her ass and legs, but, hey, Dannon had said to dress sexy. So here she was, dark eye makeup, blood red lipstick—that she hoped to leave on someone tonight—and a dress short enough to barely cover the bottom swells of her ass cheeks.

And just as the bouncer had said, Dannon sat at the bar, a drink in his hand, his eyes riveted to something behind the bar. As she drew closer, the rush of lust hit her and her body warmed. A woman sat in a chair behind the bar, the bartender's cock sliding between her big tits. Fuck. She loved this club. It was the only place in St. Louis where her kind could be open and free, and the only place she knew the humans without collars were there simply to be fucked, sucked, or drank from.

Flora slowly dragged her hand over Dannon's shoulder and squeezed his bicep. When he turned, his eyes immediately lightened as they surveyed her eyes, lips, down to the way her tits peeked out from the top of her dress, all the way to her tall heels.

"Holy shit. You did not disappoint." He leaned forward and pressed his lips to hers, his tongue sliding in to her mouth once, twice before he pulled back with a sexy smack of his lips. "You hungry?"

he asked, but by the heat in his eyes, she knew he didn't mean for food.

"Starving," she admitted, letting him take her hand to guide her through the club. Other than the raised VIP section, there was only one other section with tables reserved for special visitors. Apparently, Dannon was one of those kinds. A bouncer led them to the open table and asked if they needed anything. Dannon ordered a Crown and Coke then downed the last of the one in his hand. Flora was sort of off duty, so she ordered a Red Headed Slut.

Dannon chuckled as the bouncer hurried away. "I thought you only liked dick," he teased over her drink selection.

"Shut up, smartass," she said, pressing her lips to his and nipping his bottom lip.

Their drinks were delivered, but Flora was busy checking out the crowd; a lot of people without collars tonight. So many to choose from. "Do you see someone?" he asked, leaning close, his lips brushing her ear.

She nodded. "I see someone perfect for you," she said, turning to look in to his eyes, the glowing white of hers reflecting off the glowing gold of his.

"Show me," he said his voice deep and growly.

She pointed at the woman and heard him moan in approval. No collar meant she was free to fuck. Long, red hair. Flora couldn't see her eye color from here, but that didn't matter. What mattered were the huge tits filling the tight sparkly tank top she wore and the short black miniskirt covering a round, plump ass. She wasn't in to chicks, but if she was…she'd want a woman with curves like this one.

Dannon motioned for the bouncer and spoke in to his ear. The guy jogged off and returned with the copper-haired hottie. They invited her to sit with them and chatted her up for a few minutes, but the woman's hand kept grazing up and down Dannon's thigh. She was ready; they didn't need to seduce her.

She wanted to see this woman's mouth on Dannon's cock. Reaching down, she unzipped his pants and pulled his hard cock from his pants. Flora reached up and locked a hand around the woman's head, guiding her down to his dick.

Dannon's eyes rose to Flora's face the second the woman licked the tip of his cock. She slowly lowered her mouth on to him and Dannon growled. He grabbed Flora by the back of the neck and pulled her in roughly, shoving his tongue past her lips. She was on fire.

After a few seconds, she pulled away so she could watch. She needed to watch. It wasn't logical, but she loved the thought of seeing him like this, submissive to her. Because that was what he was right now; he was letting her set the tone, the pace, choose the woman, even choose what she would allow him to do.

Dannon leaned his head back against the seat and closed his eyes. She could see him straining to maintain his image, his façade. He couldn't reveal his true form like he could with Flora, even here. And that made her pussy heat even more. He was beautiful, the muscles straining in his neck, the vein bulging alongside. He raised a hand and placed it on top of the woman's head, pushing her faster, deeper.

Moving his other hand under the table, he slid it up Flora's thigh until he touched her pussy. Slowly, he slid one finger in to just his first knuckle, driving her need up. She shifted, forcing more of his finger inside of her, needing him to finger fuck her while she watched him get sucked off by this stranger.

Opening his eyes, he pulled the woman off his dick, pushed her away, and laid Flora along the long booth. The woman groaned a frustrated sound but crawled on top of the table and watched as Dannon shoved Flora's skirt up to her hips, plunging hard in to her.

Flora stared at the woman as she dropped her legs to Dannon's back, watched as her fingers went to her pussy as she watched them fuck. Nope, Flora wasn't into women, but this one might just change her mind. She tried to mentally will the woman to pull her top down, to free those big tits, but slammed her eyes shut as that sharp pierce of Dannon's fangs hit her shoulder.

A blinding explosion rocked through her as his lips pulled, as he sucked her blood in to his mouth, as he drank from her while fucking her. Pulling his mouth from her with a sharp scrape of his fangs, he threw his head back and roared with his release, his cock swelling and twitching inside of her, each hot jet of his cum filling her like she'd never experienced.

When Flora opened her eyes, the woman was still there, her tits hanging over her top, her head back, and her mouth open. She'd just gotten herself off watching Flora and Dannon fuck in the middle of the club.

And Flora had to remind herself once again that she was not in to women. But maybe just this one someday.

Flora lie curled in to Dannon's side as he snored lightly. They'd gone to his house for the night, although she much preferred the solitude and quiet of her house. But they were both exhausted and he just happened to live closer.

She'd fallen asleep in the car and woken as Dannon carried her through his garage. No matter how hard she fought, the bastard was just burrowing deeper and deeper.

Morning came too soon, and she groaned when her phone chimed over and over with several text messages. Dannon protested when she peeled herself from his arms and sat up, bringing her stupid phone to life.

"Oh shit," she breathed out. "Dannon. Wake up," she said. This couldn't be happening. "Dannon, are you awake?"

"Yeah. What's wrong?"

She turned her phone around for him to see the decomposing body a hunter had found in the woods. It was one of the missing pedophiles they were accusing Dannon of murdering. "Did you do this?" she asked. At this point, it didn't matter. She couldn't turn him in to her superiors even if it meant serving prison time herself.

"You still think I murdered those men?" he asked, hurt slashing through his sleepy light amber eyes. Sitting up completely, he closed his eyes and tucked his wings away, those beautiful chiseled cheekbones turned normal, his fangs shrunk in to his gums, and when he looked at her again, his eyes were brown.

"I don't care if you did. But we're going to have to come up with a good story fast."

Shaking his head, he stared at her. "You do. You think I'm the killer."

Shit. Maybe she'd been wrong and he had been innocent this whole time. A dead pedophile was the only good pedophile, but she'd accused him of taking a life. Not just any life. A human life. That generally guaranteed a death sentence. Once the trial was over and the judge declared him guilty, he'd be dragged off by the Executioner and his head would be lobbed off.

"No. I don't think you're the killer. But if there's any way this can be tied to you, we have to head this off now. Could any of your men have done it? Anyone you know? Any reason my department pegged you as the only suspect?"

His eyes drifted from her face and he shook his head as he seemed to be going over everything in his head. Finally, he looked back at her and said, "No. There's nothing and no one that I can think of. I have no idea why I was accused, but...no. I didn't kill them. Not saying I wouldn't if the situation was right, but this time, no."

Hitting her boss's number, she put the phone to her ear. It rang once before Jane answered. "Are you with him now?" she asked, her voice clipped and angry.

"Yes."

"Were you with him last night?"

Flora frowned. "Yeah. All afternoon and overnight. Why?"

Jane sighed over the phone. "That's actually good. Another sicko disappeared last night. Maybe if we can somehow connect all this shit, Dannon will be exonerated and we can move on. You'll be free to leave—"

"I'm fine here," she said, cutting off her boss.

Jane chuckled. "Yeah, well. That's what I figured." Lowering her voice, Jane said, "What's it like being mated to someone like him?"

Dannon shook his head, the bed trembling a little with his chuckle. Did Jane realize he was lying right next to her and could hear every word she said? "Interesting."

"Really? That's it?"

Another glance at Dannon and her heart stuttered. His face was so sweet, so open like he was waiting for her answer, too. "Fulfilling. Sexy. Happy." Those were the first three words that came to her mind, but, really, she could keep going. Was this normal? Were these intense feelings for him in such a short time normal? Definitely not for humans, but they weren't human. The rules were different for their kind.

Another sigh hit Flora's ears, but this time it sounded wistful. "That's what I figured. I'll call you when we get anything else." And then the call ended.

"Do you have anywhere you need to go today?" she asked. She'd have to stick to him like flies on poo until all of this was figured out.

"I'm supposed to meet Jim at Roxy's Delight. Business."

She narrowed her eyes. "What is your business exactly? Where does all your money come from?"

With a cocked brow, he smiled. "Roxy's."

"I'm sorry. What?"

"Roxy's. And PT Platinum. And Cherry Light."

She stared at him wide-eyed. "You own strip clubs?"

He rolled back when she shoved his shoulder. "What better way to ensure a constant flow of lust? And it's good money. My girls are treated with respect, have as much security as they need, dental, medical—hell, I even screen them for drugs and diseases."

"Wow," she breathed out. Now his casual demeanor and the way the waitress treated him made more sense. He was the boss. "I've never met a strip club owner," she said, leaning forward to steal a kiss. "Kind of sexy, Mr. Michaels."

She rolled off the bed and squealed when he slapped her ass. "Maybe I'll get you up on that pole someday, Officer Grumio," he called after her as she hurried for the bathroom.

Not a chance in hell would she ever be caught up on that stage with all her goodies jiggling. Now, maybe if the club was empty one day and Dannon wanted a private lap dance…

The bathroom door creaked open and she smiled a second before the curtain was pulled back. Dannon climbed in behind her and took the washcloth from her hand, washing her, pampering her. He even washed her hair. Once she was done, she stepped out to make room for him, although she'd much rather stay in there and let him pound her under the hot spray.

"When do we need to leave? Do I have time to dry my hair and eat?"

"Take all the time you want. I'll just call Jim if we're going to be late."

"Not very professional," she teased, scooting out of the way when he reached out of the shower and made a grab for her. "Stop," she squealed. "Let me finish getting ready, demon."

His chuckle followed her from the room as she jogged to the kitchen. She was going to surprise him with her lack of culinary skill. Searching the cabinets, she located bowls then sought out cereal. Of course, he'd only have kid's cereal. Pouring two bowls of Fruity Oh's, she pulled open drawers, looking for spoons.

And instead found a Sig Sauer P-226. An odd choice, and an even odder hiding place, but she pushed the drawer shut and kept looking. Why did he have a gun in the kitchen? It wasn't exactly weird that he'd carry being as he travelled at night a lot. Humans weren't the dangerous ones anymore. But why in the kitchen?

And why was she making such a big deal about it? Are you trying to find something wrong with him? Because so far, he was damned near perfect for her.

Dannon's steps moved away from her as he headed to get dressed. She quickly poured the milk and stood proudly behind the bowls and waited for him to join her. He was gone for too long. She glanced at the loops in the bowl and wondered how long it would be before they got soggy.

"Dannon?" she called. "I made breakfast."

He didn't answer. With a frown, she jogged down the hall. "Hey," she said, turning the corner in to his bedroom.

But he was looking at his phone with an angry frown between his brows, his eyes glowing that bright gold. "Do you know Kian?" he asked, his eyes turning up to her.

She shrugged. "Not well. Why?"

He turned his phone and showed a picture of her naked, head thrown back, eyes closed. "What the fuck?" she breathed out, taking the phone from his hand. "He sent this to you?"

"Yeah. When was that?" His voice was doing that deep, growly thing.

Frowning down at him, she tilted her head. "Now you're jealous? I've never slept with Kian, Dannon. I'm not even sure who this is," she said, spreading her fingers on the screen to enlarge the picture. At least it was a flattering one of her, but she couldn't tell who'd taken it by the odd angle. "I don't know who that is."

"You don't remember your picture being taken?" She shook her head. "Do you recognize the bedding?"

"Yeah. That's mine. Was mine. I replaced it a couple months back. The fabric was itchy," she said, still studying the picture. "How the hell would the vamp Prince get hold of it? And why the fuck did he send it to you? To make you jealous?" she said with a snort. The fucker better not be jealous after what they'd shared last night. He hadn't finished with that girl, but he sure as hell seemed to be enjoying himself.

Dannon shook his head. "I don't know how he got it, and I don't know why he'd send it." He reached for his phone and enlarged the picture until it was just her filling the screen. "But I'm going to find out."

Soggy cereal forgotten, Flora twisted her hair into a messy bun on top of her head and pulled on a tank top and jeans. Dannon smiled and ran his finger lightly over her marks. He loved when she showed them off, and why not put it out there now when they were heading in to a building full of horny men?

His buddy, Jim, was waiting for him outside when they pulled up in Flora's car. He'd suggested they ride his bike, but she was scared. Someday. She definitely wanted to be on the back of that thing someday, her arms wrapped around his waist as he sped down the highway. But not today. Today, she was all about self-preservation and getting across the river in one piece so she could get as much info about Dannon's life and job as possible. Maybe something she learned could help clear his name from the suspect list.

Dannon talked low with Jim while Flora looked around the room. A few dancers avoided her eyes while a couple of them smiled and waved. One woman, more like a girl, came off the stage and made a beeline for her. "Hi. I'm Jem. Well, not really, but yeah. I just wanted to meet the boss's new wife."

"We're not—"

"Thanks, Jem. That's nice of you," Dannon said, cutting Flora's protests off.

When Jem bounced away, her bare ass jiggling with every step, Dannon turned to her. "Did you already forget about these?" he said, his fingers grazing those marks again. This time, it sent a shiver up her spine.

Oh yeah. Maybe there was no ceremony or piece of paper from the judge, but yeah…they were kind of married now. Whoa. She was a wife? "Does that make you my husband?" she asked, her heart picking up its pace when his hand found her inner thigh under the table.

"Hmmm … I like that. Say it again."

"Whatever you want, husband," she teased, batting her eyes.

Dannon leaned in for a kiss, but was interrupted by a very obvious clearing of a throat. When they pulled apart, that asshole Kian, prince of the Midwest vamps, second runner up to a nest of jackasses, stood in front of their table, his entourage not far behind. "Did you receive my text?" he asked, his eyes moving to Flora. He looked her up and down, his eyes hesitating on her breasts before zeroed in on her mark. "Ah. I see you've marked her anyway. So, this is an open arrangement?" Kian said, moving closer to where Flora sat.

"No. It's not," Dannon growled out. His hand tightened on her thigh.

"Where did you get that pic?" Flora asked, reaching under the table to pry his fingers from her before he snapped her damn femur.

Kian shrugged. "I've seen a few of them. You do like being photographed, though."

"What?" Not once had she ever allowed anyone to take a picture or video of her when she was naked. That was the best way to end up all over Facebook or some free porn site. "You're a fucking liar."

A man stepped forward, his wide shoulders dwarfing the prince. Two men moved in from the sides of the club, their eyes on the group surrounding the prince. One of them glanced at Dannon, who shook his head. These were Dannon's elusive soldiers. She'd yet to see any photo evidence of them, but had heard so many stories of how far Dannon's influence reached.

"I think it's time to go," Dannon said, his voice calm, but he still had that vice like grip on her leg. Was he trying to keep her in the booth or himself?

"Very well. Miss Grumio, hope to see you again soon." He nodded his head as if he were bowing and stepped beside the behemoth who'd moved in behind him. That son of a bitch actually glared at her.

"Please, by all means, do something. I'll have you locked up so fast your ugly head will spin." Did these assholes not know she was a fucking cop?

The behemoth chuckled, but the smile didn't quite reach his eyes. "See you around, little girl."

As they filed out the door, the two men she'd noticed moving closer, as well as four men who sat around the tables, stood and followed them out. "Were they all yours?" she asked.

He nodded, but his glowing eyes were on the spot where Kian had disappeared. "Hey," she said, cupping his face and turning him so he had to look at her. "I appreciate you jumping to defend my honor," she said. He nuzzled against her hand. "But maybe next time do it without strangling my leg."

His hand jerked from her and he stared at his hand as if he'd forgotten he had one. "I'm sorry," he said, his eyes raising to hers. "That mother fucker just rubs me the wrong way every time he's around."

"I get it. He's a douche nozzle." That earned her a smile and a kiss.

Now that the drama had passed, it was time to get to work. Flora sat back and listened to everything, asked questions about dates, even got him to tell her a little more about the guards positioned throughout the club. He paid them, yeah, but they were there because they were loyal. That was as far as he would go with that. It didn't matter; he'd given her quite a bit. But still not enough to get him off the hook with the cops.

Prince Fucking Kian. That asshole had an agenda, but for the life of him, Dannon couldn't figure it out. He didn't need Flora; he had chicks throwing themselves at his feet day and night. He was just trying to piss Dannon off. One more fucking incident and the prick was barred from any of his clubs, consequences be damned.

Flora leaned in to his side and listened as he went over his books with Jim. She'd genuinely seemed surprised and a little pissed about the picture. He believed her. What reason would she have to lie? Kian sure as fuck didn't seem like the kind of guy she'd go for. He was a fucking weasel. Arrogant. Full of himself for no other fucking reason than his family's power and money.

And he realized how many times he'd used the word fuck in the few minutes he'd thought about Asshole Kian. His guys came back in, chuckling, and his lead guy lifted his hand and gave him a thumbs up. He knew they hadn't touched the Prince; that would cause a fucking war with their people. But no reason they couldn't fuck with his bodyguards a little.

His lead guy, Mattie, came over to the table. He leaned down and put his mouth to his ear. "Keep her close. Something's up."

"She can hear you," Flora whispered back. "And she's a cop."

Mattie jerked up, his eyes wide. A smile pulled up his lips and Dannon looked over at Flora. Her eyes were glowing and she'd allowed her fangs to drop in to her mouth. "Well then. Guess you should keep an eye on him," Mattie said, turning and sauntering back to his seat at one of the four stages. It was slow enough in the day that he'd blend in to the crowd when they started packing in after dark.

Keep her close. Was Kian after Flora for real? Was that what this was all about? Was that why he'd sent Dannon the picture; to send him away in a jealous fit? Guess vamps didn't know much about his Incubi.

And if Kian thought for one second he'd share his mate with a piece of shit vampire, the mother fucker was about to learn a hard lesson.

Chapter Six

"I have to go in to the precinct. Think you can stay out of trouble for a few hours?" Flora asked as Dannon watched her dress.

"Whyyyy?" he whined. "Stay in bed with me today. Let's be irresponsible and blow off work."

Leaning across the bed, she laid her head on his chest and listened to his heart lightly thump through his chest. "I have to go in or you go to jail. And I don't think Missouri allows conjugal visits. You don't want me out there letting men mark me every day, now do you?" A low growl worked up his chest. "That's what I thought." She kissed the warm skin over his left pec and pushed to her feet.

"What are you doing today?"

"Leading Moore on a wild ride."

Flora giggled and frowned. "What do you mean?"

He shrugged. "A long boring day of accountants, meeting with bankers, you know…the exciting criminal life."

She stared at him, his hair tousled from the wild sex they had then the short sleep they'd gotten. She had a hard time picturing Dannon Michaels sitting at a desk with an accountant. But he was a business man, even if he was a sexy, rugged one. "I'll call you when I'm done."

Flora leaned over for one last kiss and left him in bed. They'd taken turns sleeping at each other's house for the last three weeks. It had been almost two weeks since she'd learned of his interesting occupation. It was brilliant, though. She'd gotten almost lust drunk sitting with him one night when a fraternity filed in and threw hundreds of dollar bills at the beautiful women Dannon hired.

Stepping in to the bright sun, Flora slid her sunglasses over her eyes and frowned. A motor idled a half block down. When she turned to look at it, it sped away, its license plate missing. Running to her car, she fumbled with her stupid key fob, then climbed in and started the engine. She pulled her seat belt in place as she raced down the street. Hitting Dannon's number, she put it on speaker.

"You miss me already," he said, his voice deep.

"Have you noticed a navy colored sedan hanging out lately? Parked outside your house or down the block?"

The line was silent for a few beats. Dannon sighed. "No. Why?"

"This is the second time I've seen this car outside your house, and, both times, it fled when it noticed me watching."

"You're chasing it now, aren't you?" he asked. She could hear fabric rustling in the background.

"I'm trying to find it. It turned the corner before I could get in my piece of shit car. Come on!" she yelled as someone pulled in front of her, causing her to slam on her brakes.

"Hold on and I'll catch up to you."

"No you won't. You'll stay there and stay out of trouble. This is my job, Dannon. And you're my husband. I won't let you dig yourself further in to trouble because you forget that I'm not a weak, fragile female."

He growled, but this time it was a frustrated sound. "I don't think you're a weak, fragile female, but like you said, you are my wife and I'd rather you not rush in to something unknown and alone. Where the fuck is Moore?"

"I don't know. Call him and tell him what's up. I'm heading south on Baymont Street. I'm hanging up and calling this in." She hesitated. She really didn't know who she was chasing or what she'd find if she caught the guy. This could very well be their last conversation. "Dannon…"

"Yeah," he said, his voice full of concern.

"I love you," she said, ending the call before he could say anything else. She needed him to know that, just in case. She'd seen enough men and women in uniform killed to know most people didn't get to say goodbye. She wouldn't be one of those. She might not have said a farewell, but he would know how she felt if she went down.

Where the fuck was that sedan? How fast was the fucker driving to get through a subdivision this quickly? Then again, he could've turned the opposite way she did.

Hitting Jane's number, she propped her phone between her shoulder and cheek. "Dannon called," Jane said as a greeting. "Did you find the sedan?"

"No." She slowed her vehicle and pulled off to the side. "Fuck. I think I lost it. This is the second time, Chief."

"You sure it's the same vehicle?"

"Yeah; it's the same. Both times, it took off when the driver spotted me. Someone's watching Dannon."

"I bet they are. Another victim was located."

Shit. Not good news. "Why didn't you text me?"

"Because his almost completely decomposed body was found hanging from a tree in the woods about forty miles from where the first body was found."

"Suicide?" she asked hopefully.

"That's how it's being written up for now. Are you on your way in?"

"I was until that fucker led me on a wild goose chase."

"Has Dannon noticed it before today?"

"No. I already asked him."

"I don't know what to say. Come in and we'll see if we can't narrow this down. There are a shit ton of sedans on the road."

"There was a small white scuff of paint on the passenger side rear bumper."

"Still doesn't narrow it down. We'll go through the records and see if anyone in a white vehicle reported a fender bender with a blue or black sedan. See you soon." Chief Jarbo ended the call.

"Fuck!" Flora yelled in to the empty car.

Why did it seem like someone was setting Dannon up for all of this? She knew from the get-go something was off about the whole thing, but now that she knew Dannon inside and out, she knew one hundred percent he had nothing to do with the murders or disappearances. Instincts told her whoever was in that blue car knew something, and she'd find him before he caused any more damage to her man's reputation.

Several cars littered the parking lot of her precinct. Flora shoved her door open and stomped across the parking lot, her earlier

68

good mood all but gone. When she found the asshole responsible for all of this, she was going to personally hand him over to the Executioner. While she didn't really care that a couple of pedophiles and rapists were no longer breathing the same air as her, she didn't like the fact someone was doing everything in their power to make it look like Dannon had a hand in it.

The receptionist, Caren, was just leaving Chief Jarbo's office when Flora neared it. The Fairy smiled and winked at Flora as she passed, but Flora just shook her head. Nope. Still not in to chicks.

"Why was Dannon implicated?" she asked, turning and slamming the door. "What made the department look at him to begin with? What evidence was there to suspect him in the disappearances?"

Jane leaned back in her chair, her eyes a bright green as she studied Flora. "Sit," she ordered, reaching in to a drawer of her desk and pulling a manila file out. She opened it and pushed it toward Flora.

There were dozens of pictures, and Dannon was in every single one. In each, there was a different man, Dannon in his face, his mouth open as if he were talking or yelling, his eyes blazing a bright gold, his fangs present, and the man seemed to be cowering from him. As she flipped through, she realized every single one of the men Dannon was confronting was the men who'd gone missing.

"Is this outside of his clubs?" Flora asked, flipping from one picture to the next.

"Yes. And each of those men went missing the same night those pictures were taken."

"Wait...if he was only just accused, why was someone photographing him?"

When Jane didn't respond, Flora looked up. "We didn't take these."

With a deep frown between her brows, she looked back at the pictures in her hands. "Then who did?"

"That, we don't know. But those were sent to us after a few missing persons reports had been filed by family, friends, or coworkers."

"Son of a bitch," Flora breathed out. "And no one thought this might be a set up?"

"Actually, a few of us did. But, as of right now, he's literally the only person with any connection to all seven of those men. He's the last person to see them before they disappeared."

"Unless whoever sent these pics was the last person," Flora said, closing the file and tossing it on top of Jane's desk. "Fuck." Rubbing her temples with the pads of her fingers, Flora tried to go over the very little they'd learned since she'd been assigned to Dannon. Even in the time since they'd been mated, there was still little to clear his name. He was at the club on each night the men went missing. And according to these pictures, so were the victims. Right back to square one.

"Who's with Dannon today?"

"Moore. I figured you'd approve."

Yeah; she did. Moore didn't hold any prejudices against her mate. Hell. He seemed to have a bit of a crush on him, so that could end up working on her behalf if anything went down. "Okay." She breathed deeply. "Okay. I'm going to my desk. I'm going to make some more phone calls. I'll figure this out."

"Good luck," Jane said with a shake of her head. "Because I've spent way too many hours on it. The victims' families haven't changed their stories. No one remembers anything out of place or received any suspicious calls or packages. No emails or odd messages on anyone's computers or their social media pages."

"I'll find something," Flora said, standing and reaching for the door. "I have to." She stepped back in to the area containing cubicles and desks and inhaled deeply. There were sounds of fingers hitting keyboards, a phone ringing somewhere to her left, there were two others talking to her right, someone was moaning near the stair well. This was her second home; this is where she thought the most clearly, and where she got the most done.

Pulling her chair out, she dropped heavily and wiggled her mouse to bring the computer screen to life. She'd figure it out. She would. There was no way she'd let her husband go down for a crime he didn't commit, even it meant fleeing the fucking country.

After six hours, Flora was no further than she was when she'd sat. Most of the families were irritated with her repeated questions. They'd already told other detectives the same fucking things, but still, she had to make sure there was no stone unturned.

"Hey," Jane said, stepping behind her and leaning her hip against Flora's desk. "I didn't know you were still here."

Leaning back, Flora looked up at her boss. "Yep. And got zero done. I might as well have played solitaire all day for the progress I made."

Jane's hand gripped Flora's shoulder and squeezed a little. "Go home, Flora."

Politely shrugging from Jane's grip, she leaned forward and shut down her computer. "I'm going to the club. Dannon texted a while ago and said he'd be working all night. Feel like a night out?"

"Hey, Caren," Jane called out, looking over Flora's head.

Well shit. She hadn't meant a fucking girl's night. She barely knew Caren, and wasn't looking forward to getting stuck with her and Jane all night. But she didn't want to be a bitch and rescind her invite now.

"Yeah," Caren said, peeking her head around the corner.

"What time do you get off?"

Caren smiled and lowered her lashes. "Anytime you want me to."

"She meant want time do you clock out?" Flora shook her head, but she couldn't help the smile. They bantered like Dannon and Flora did. Maybe there was more to them than just a little workplace nookie.

"Oh. In about ten minutes. Why?" She stepped fully in to the center of the room.

"We're going out." Jane looked down at Flora. "Where are we going?"

"He's at Roxy's Delight tonight."

"Roxy's Delight," Jane said to Caren. The receptionist might be in the other category, but she didn't have the same hearing as Succubae like Jane and Flora.

"I'm in," she said, hurrying back to her desk. Flora could hear fabric rustling and drawers opening and closing. A few minutes later, Caren returned wearing a bright pink tank top and her lips and eyes had been darkened.

"You always keep a change of clothes here?" Flora asked, rolling her chair back and standing.

"Yep. Never know when a girl might want some fun after work."

The drive to Roxy's Delight took close to thirty minutes, and Caren rambled the whole time. The woman was the epitome of office busybody. She knew everything about everyone and had no problem telling secrets. Flora made a mental note to never confide in the petite Fairy.

The parking lot of Roxy's was full so Flora had to park at the very back of the lot. Well shit. At least she was wearing tennis shoes instead of heels. Caren, on the other hand, had slipped on a pair of stilettos and groaned when she realized how far she'd have to walk.

"Do you want me to drop you off at the door?" Flora said with a roll of her eyes.

"Would you? I'd be sooo grateful," Caren said, leaning on the back of Flora's seat.

With a sigh of utter frustration, Flora pulled along the front of the building and waited for Caren and Jane to climb out. "You're both getting out? You're going to make me walk by myself?"

"You're a cop. She's not."

"It's not like I can bring my gun in there, Jane."

"You're also a Succubus. She's just a little Fairy," Jane said with a smile as she swung the door shut.

In other words, she wanted to be with Caren instead of walking through the crowded parking lot. Shoving her gun and badge in to the glove compartment, she pushed her door open and climbed out. Hitting the lock button on her fob, she shook her head as she started her hike to where her man was waiting.

From the distance, she could hear the thump of the bass and could see Caren and Jane standing just outside the entrance. Jane had an arm around Caren's shoulders and said something in to the Fairy's ear, making her throw her head back and laugh.

"Miss Grumio," a male voice said from her right. Turning her head, she groaned as she spotted Kian and his merry band of assholes following. There were only three of them with Kian tonight, but that behemoth asshole who'd seemed intent on threatening her last time was a step behind the vampire prince.

"Prince Kian," she replied, her voice emotionless. She kept walking, no intention of engaging the asshole after he'd found it necessary to send a picture of her fucking someone else to her new husband.

"Miss Grumio," Kian called. "Flora, wait."

With a huff of air, Flora stopped and waited for Kian to catch up. "What?"

"I just wanted to apologize for last time. I was rude. We were rude," he said, jerking his head toward the behemoth. "Tomas, apologize."

"Sorry," Tomas the giant said, a cold smile on his lips.

"Great. Apology accepted." Flora turned and started walking again, but a tight hand on her bicep pulled her to a stop. "What, Kian?"

She tugged at her arm but his grip was tight. Damn. Vampires were stronger than she'd realized. "I just want to talk."

"About what?" Again, she tugged at her arm. She really didn't want to have to start a fight with the Prince and risk all kinds of fallout from his family.

He finally released her arm and held his hands out in front of him. "About you?"

She shook her head and crossed her arms over her chest, kept her peripheral vision on the men now spreading out and surrounding her. Shit. Her weapon was in the car and there was no way she could take on all four of them at once. She was good for one or two, tops.

"I know you and Dannon are now mated, but I've heard through the grapevine you two are still open to further relationships."

"Well, you heard wrong." Why the fuck was he all about Flora now? She'd barely met him a time or two and now he wanted her? He could buy just about any woman he wanted, but not her.

"Were you two not at Club D?"

"Of course we were. Not that it's any of your business."

"Ah. So you're just not open to me."

Was that hurt that flashed through Kian's eyes? Not that she cared, but why? "Look, Prince Kian—"

"Please, just Kian."

With a roll of her eyes, she shook her head. "Fine, Kian. You seem like a nice guy. You're good looking. Find someone not already mated. I'm not interested."

Once again, she turned to walk away, but Tomas blocked her path. "Do you disrespect your prince?"

"Tomas," Kian said, warning in his voice.

Dropping her hands to her sides and preparing for a fight, she dipped her head a little to inventory where everyone else was. "He's not my Prince. I'm not a vamp. Please move."

He crossed his arms over his massive chest and stared down his nose at her. Flora stepped to the side, but the fucker followed. "I don't want any trouble."

"Then I suggest you bow to your prince and accept his offer."

"Tomas, leave her alone. Let her go," Kian said, taking a step closer but still staying far enough away that he'd be no good.

"Fuck you," Flora said a second before she pulled her fist back and let it fly. She got one hit in before the others jumped in.

"Enough!" Kian bellowed, but his guards didn't stop.

She held her own for a few seconds, able to dodge and parry effectively. She was a full-blooded Succubus and was stronger and faster than vampires.

But there were three of them and just her.

"Hey!" a female screamed from across the parking lot as she took a blow to the side of her head.

Flora moved quickly to avoid the second hit and swung out her leg, taking down one of the smaller guards.

Feet thundered toward her, but she couldn't pull her eyes from the men in front of her lest they take her down. Someone wrapped an arm around her throat from behind, but he was pulled off her, the move pulling her back and down. The second she hit the ground, she immediately pushed back to her feet. If she stayed down, they'd overpower her in a second.

But she was no longer fighting alone. Dannon, Jim, Jane, and Joe were now in the fray. The big fucker, Tomas, was on the ground, silver handcuffs snapped around his wrist with Jane holding him down with a foot on his back.

"You dare touch my fucking wife?" Dannon bellowed out, lunging at Kian.

Flora stepped in his way and shoved him back. They didn't need to start a war between their kind and Kian's. There were far more vamps than Succubae and Incubi since vamps could turn humans while her kind could only be born.

"He didn't touch me," Flora said, trying to calm her man before things went way worse.

"Release my guard," Kian insisted. Not once had he actually tried to enter the fight. He'd attempted to stop it, although he'd never actually physically got in the way of his guards' swinging fists.

"He's under arrest for assaulting an officer of the St. Louis Paranormal Police. Unless you want to go down with him, I suggest you back the fuck off." Jane. Hell yeah. Her boss was a bit of a badass. This was the first time Flora had actually seen her in action and now she knew how she'd climbed to her position.

Prince Kian smirked and backed away. "Let's go," he ordered the last two guards who were now posturing toward Dannon and Mattie.

They didn't turn their backs on her group until they were far enough away, then climbed in to an expensive Town Car and sped off, their tires screaming on the asphalt.

"Shit," Flora said, bending and planting her hands on her knees.

"You okay?" Dannon said, running his hand over her hair, moving it to the side to check out the lump she knew was there. The whole side of her fucking head was throbbing, but it would be healed within a few hours.

"Yeah. I'm fine. Thanks," she said, straightening her spine.

"Caren came running in screaming like a banshee that someone was trying to kill you," Joe said, helping Jane pull Tomas to his feet.

"We weren't trying to kill the bitch," Tomas said. Joe's foot shot out and hooked Tomas's foot. He went down hard.

"Oops," Joe said, pulling him back to his feet. Flora had no doubt Tomas would run in to a few walls before he was finally locked behind silver bars.

"You sure you're okay?" Dannon asked, running his hands up and down her bare arms.

"I'm a cop, Dannon. I've been through worse," she said, but pressed her lips to his to lessen the sting of her tone of voice. "Thank you. I think I was outnumbered."

"Just a little," he said, holding his hand up and pushing his thumb and forefinger together until there was just an inch between them.

Dannon threw his arm around Flora and led her inside with Jim flanking her other side. Both of them seemed to be scanning the parking lot as they made their way to the building, as if they were looking for more trouble.

The club was packed, and Caren waited just inside the door with Mattie standing behind her, large arms crossed over his barrel chest. "How about next time you let Jim babysit the Fairy and let me kick some ass?" he growled out, his eyes a bright amber. Not an Incubus. Shifter perhaps? It would explain his massive size.

"Next time," Dannon teased.

"Thanks," Caren said, turning and patting Mattie's forearm. The large male's face softened a little as he dipped his head at Caren. "Where's Jane?" she asked, looking over Flora's shoulder.

"She and Joe are taking one of those fuckers to the precinct," Flora said.

"Do you want me to get you a ride home? You're welcome to stay here," Dannon said. "Drinks are on the house for saving my wife."

"Yeah, some help I was," Caren grumbled, crossing her thin arms under her perky tits.

"Hey. If it weren't for you, we wouldn't have known anything was going on."

"You couldn't have fought them," Flora said. "I appreciate your help, but they would've taken you down in a second. What good would that have been?" She smiled at Caren in hopes of infusing a little humor in to the situation.

"Whatever. I hate being so fucking weak."

Jim gently took Caren by the elbow and escorted her further in to the club. Flora and Dannon followed. So much lust filled the room Flora felt almost drunk. "Damn," she breathed out as a wave hit her, making her sway on her feet.

Dannon lifted his chin, gesturing toward one of the stages on the far wall. There were two strippers on one stage and they were slowly undressing each other, their hands cupping each other's tits, rubbing their glistening bodies against each other. They were covered in some kind of oil.

"The frat boys love a little girl on girl," Dannon said in Flora's ear, waving his hand for her to lower in to a booth before him, a wall on her right. It wasn't lost on her that he put himself between her and the rest of the room.

"I think everyone loves to watch a little girl on girl," Flora said, leaning in to Dannon when he lifted his arm and draped it over the back of the booth.

"Hmmm. I'd love to see you in a little girl on girl."

"You can keep dreaming. I'm strictly dick, remember?" she teased. She'd said that to him the first time she'd followed him here.

With a chuckle, Dannon dipped his head and stole a kiss. "That scared the shit out of me," he admitted, looking in to her eyes. His were glowing her favorite gold, his beast just on the surface. "It felt like I was running in a dream. Like everything had slowed down and I wouldn't get to you."

"I don't think they were going to kill me. They were just trying to scare me in to letting the Prince…"

"Letting the prince what?" he asked, his voice deeper, his fangs slowly dropping through his gums.

"First of all, you better calm down unless you want everyone to see your true form. And he said he wanted…actually, he never said anything exactly. Just said he'd heard we had an open arrangement, like he had last time he was here, and it sounded like he wanted a go at me."

"So, he wants to fuck you," Dannon said, pushing his hand through his hair and breathing deeply. The next time he opened his eyes, they were back to the brown of his humanoid form.

"Sounds like it. When I turned him down, his buddies went all macho. Wouldn't let me pass. I slugged the big dude, and that's around the time you came in to the picture."

Shaking his head over and over, he kept staring at her. "You know I don't care who you sleep with," he said.

"Ew. Kian would be the last one on my list. Zero attraction to him. He's too…pompous or something." She glanced up as a man as tall as Dannon walked by them and stepped in to the bathroom. His shoulders were wide, his back broad, and he had that designer beard thing going on. "Now him, I'd fuck," she teased.

Chapter Seven

Flora let Dannon walk her to her car and demanded Joe follow her back to her house. "This is ridiculous, Dannon," she said.

"Yeah, I know you're a cop, but this will at least make me feel better. Besides, it'll be another couple of hours before I can leave here. Joe can ease some of your…discomfort."

"You're dirty," she said, lifting on to her tiptoes to press her lips to his. When she pulled back, she smiled. "What about you?"

He looked around and shrugged. "I'm sure I can find someone."

Since they'd shared that experience at Club D, neither of them had been with another person. Hell; they'd spent so much time together they could just do each other when the need arose.

"Don't be long," she teased, nipping his bottom lip and pressing her hand against his crotch. He was hard and ready, the length filling her with heat. "Mmmm … now I don't want to leave."

He pushed his hips forward once, but pulled her in for a hug instead of dragging her to the back room. Damn. The drama earlier really had affected him more than she'd realized. Danger was nothing new to Flora; it was part of her job. Of course, she'd have preferred to have been armed when they'd decided to play Billy Badass with a smaller female, but she'd done okay for a few minutes.

"Go home, take a long, hot shower, and crawl in to bed naked. I'll be home as soon as I can."

Home. It was her house, but it was their home. Same with his house. Maybe it was time to talk about moving in together. Such a major step, but, hell, they were married in the eyes of their kind. Might as well combine their assets and live in one house. It was going to suck to let him know she wouldn't be moving in to the suburbs any time soon.

Dannon wrapped his hand in her hair and pulled her close, his lips hard as they pressed against hers; it was a needy, desperate kiss. Why? She was safe. She was in one piece and standing right in front of him, her body pressed along the length of his. He'd have to get over this kind of reaction to her in harm's way real fast, because there was no way she'd ever quit working.

Joe waited just inside the entranceway, his arms crossed over his chest, his eyes moving around the room. She sometimes forgot how big of a badass he really was. It was hard to see him in that light when he was always flirting and joking about sex. But now? Now he was in full protector mode. Now he was a cop. Now he was ready to crack skulls.

"You ready?" she asked when she neared him.

He nodded once, his eyes hard. Pushing the door open, Flora stepped in to the stuffy summer evening and hurried to her car. She really was ready to go home. Those fuckers had almost ruined her night, but at least one of them would be sleeping on the hard concrete of the jail cell deep inside the precinct basement.

Joe's headlights were so close he was damned near riding her bumper the entire way to her house. When she pulled up her driveway and parked along the back, he was out of his car and at her side before she could pull her house keys from her pocket.

The second they were inside, Joe was on her, his hands on her face, in her hair, his fingers rough as they jerked her clothes away. "I thought…" he groaned out, his voice deep and guttural like Dannon's got when he was closer to losing control. "You're my best friend," he said, yanking her shirt over his head. "I can't ever lose you, Flora."

This was the most emotion, true emotion she'd ever seen from her friend and coworker. She had no idea she meant so much to him, although maybe it should've been obvious.

With trembling hands, he undid her pants and pushed them down her legs, then bent and scooped her up. Then he surprised her by slamming his mouth over hers, his teeth pressing against the delicate flesh almost to the point of pain.

Joe was going to fuck her to show her how much she meant to him. She knew even before they started that Joe would mark her. He'd leave his scent on her. It was a baser need; something deep inside of him that needed to make sure she was here with him.

80

Pulling his mouth from hers, Joe laid her on the couch and followed her down, pushing her legs apart with rough hands. And as he slid in to her, she realized how much she needed this from him. Sex didn't equal love to her kind, but it was a connection. A way of showing dominance, relations, or a bond. Pixies might not mate the same way her kind did, but he obviously needed the touch.

His thrusts were hard and hurried as he dipped his head and took one of her nipples in to his mouth. Sucking on one until it was a hard bud, he pulled away and slanted his mouth over hers again. His tongue darted in to her mouth as he hooked a hand under her knee and spread her more for him, pounding in to her as if he could fill her with everything he couldn't say.

Before she had the chance to come, Joe groaned, pulled his dick from her, and yanked on it, his milky cum hitting her stomach and tits. "Mine," he ground out. She stared up at him, reveling in the fact that, just like Dannon, he'd dropped his shield and revealed his true form to her.

His ears came to a point, barely peeking through his shoulder length hair. His eyes were a bright green, almost the color of grass, and his pupils were tiny pinpoints in the center. Tiny, little pointy wings sprouted from his back as spurt after spurt hit her bare flesh.

When he finished, he sat back on his knees and stared down at her. "I know you're a bad ass, Flora. And I'm not trying to be a pig, but, next time, wait for one of us to at least even the playing field."

Leaning forward, he pressed a light kiss to her forehead and stood, heading down her hall. He knew her house inside and out with as many times as he'd visited her. He returned with a clean towel and gently cleaned his jizz from her skin. "Dannon's going to be pissed," he said with a smile, shaking his head as he tried to get as much off her as possible.

"No he won't. He suggested we fuck," Flora said, taking her shirt from Joe's outstretched hand. As she pulled it on, he tugged her pants up her legs. "Don't bother. I'm getting in the shower before he gets home, anyway."

"Thought you said he wouldn't be pissed," Joe teased.

81

"That we fucked? No. That you marked me and declared me yours?" She shook her head.

"Yeah. I said that, didn't I?"

Flora giggled a little, feeling heady. "It's fine, Joe. I get it."

"You want me to wait until Dannon gets home?"

"If you want, but I'm fine."

His wings and tips of his ears hadn't disappeared yet, so she figured his emotions were still high. When he stretched out on the couch after she stood, she just shook her head with a chuckle. She didn't need him here, but, apparently, he did. He needed to make sure she was still safe until her husband got home. A little chauvinistic, but as she'd experienced earlier, it was always good to have a little backup.

After a skin reddening hot shower, Flora climbed in to bed, naked, just as Dannon had requested. She wondered if Joe would leave once Dannon got home, but only thought about it for a few seconds until sleep dragged her under. When she woke next, Dannon was already between her legs and pumping in to her.

Damn. She loved waking up like this. Reaching forward, she pulled him down and reveled in the feeling of his wings as she ran her fingers up and down his back. Even in the dark, even with her eyes closed, she knew his touch, knew his scent, knew his essence.

She was still half-asleep when he pulled from her and laid on top of her, wedging his cock between them. He swelled and twitched as his hot cum coated her stomach. His lips found hers in the dark as he marked her with his seed, then rolled over and pulled her head on to his chest. The dampness on her belly was cool until he pulled the blanket over both their bodies and hugged her tightly.

That made two men in her life who'd marked her in one night. But Dannon's would stay until she showered the next day, his scent covering her for hours.

When she woke the next morning, someone had opened the curtains in her bedroom and the sun spilled over her bed, creating an orange glow behind her lids. She groaned and rolled over, pulling the blanket over her head.

"Time to get up," Joe said as the bed shifted with his weight.

Yanking the blanket down, she stared up at him. "You're still here?"

He nodded and offered her a cup of steaming coffee. "Yep. Dannon told me to hang out with you for a little while longer."

"Oh, for fuck's sake," she growled out, kicking the blankets off. "I carry a gun, too, Joe. And I'm a Succubus. I could kick your ass if I wanted."

"Agreed. But two are better than one."

"Yeah, yeah," she said, rolling her eyes at his pathetic excuse.

Joe followed her to the bathroom and leaned against the door frame as she turned the water on and let it heat up. His eyes roamed her body and he reached down to shift his boner to the other side. "Not now, Joe," she said. She wasn't in the mood for dick. She wanted a shower, coffee, and food, in that order. "Where did Dannon go?" she asked, lifting a foot to step in to the tub.

"That navy sedan was in your driveway last night," he said. She froze with her hand on the curtain and yanked it back open.

"What? Why didn't he wake me up? Why didn't you?"

He shrugged. "Because the Chief sent a couple of cars out last night. They couldn't find him, but they're still out looking. So is Dannon."

"Joe!" she screeched in an angry voice. Shutting the water off, she jogged from the bathroom. "This is our fucking job."

"Not this morning. Right now, my job is keeping you in the house."

"What?" she asked, turning on him as she pulled her jeans up her hips. "What the fuck does that mean?"

"Your mate seems to think the car is after you, not him. It was at the end of the driveway when he pulled up. He got out and tried to approach it, but they drove through your yard and took off. They tore your yard up a little, by the way."

Yanking a shirt over her head, she threw her hands in the air. "Why would they be after me? I saw them outside of Dannon's house."

"Yeah, but Dannon wasn't here when they showed up."

"They didn't know that." She sat on the end of her bed and jerked on her tennis shoes, not bothering to tie the laces.

"Or maybe they did. You ever wonder who took those pictures, Flora? It wasn't anyone from our department. Maybe someone has been trailing him long before we came in to the picture."

"So, what do I have to do with any of this?" She sat up and watched Joe; saw the look flash through his eyes. "Joe," she said, her voice more forceful.

"I don't know. Dannon thinks someone might be after you, like Kian. Or maybe they want to use you to get to him. I really don't know. But...I told you, you're my best friend. I won't be responsible for you getting killed because you think it's your job to save the world."

"Still doesn't make sense. They were trying to frame Dannon long before I came in to the..." And then it hit her. She hadn't been the original target, but now that she was close to Dannon, they could use her as bait or something, like Joe had said. If they could get her away from Dannon, threaten her life, maybe he'd crack and do something stupid...like attack the Prince of the Vamps. "Son of a bitch," she muttered.

"What?" Joe asked, moving out of the way as she left her bedroom.

"I'd bet my fucking wings this is all Kian. He's the one doing all this."

"Why do you think that?"

She told him about the pictures Jane had shown her, about the picture Kian had sent to Dannon, about what Kian said to her outside. While it wasn't exactly a smoking gun, maybe now they had something to go on.

Her front door opened and closed, and Flora turned to see Dannon step in to her living room. "You had Joe stay here and babysit me? Really? This is my fucking job, Dannon."

"And it's my fucking job to protect you." He stood there with his arms crossed over his chest, his eyes blazing that bright gold as he stared at her.

"She thinks Kian is behind all of this," Joe said, his tone light as if he were trying to break the current mood.

"I agree," Dannon said, but his eyes never left Flora's face.

"Is there something else you want to say to me?" Flora asked as he continued to glare at her.

"Yesterday, when you took off after that sedan, why did you say that?"

"Say what?"

"You said you loved me and hung up. Why?"

Well shit. She inhaled deeply and closed her eyes for a second. If she admitted why she'd said that, it would only make both Dannon and Joe more nervous. And she refused to give up her job, regardless of how much she loved them both.

"In case I didn't have the chance to say goodbye."

"So, you said that in case that was our last conversation? And you still wonder why I'm so fucking protective? Hell. You got your best friend so freaked out, he felt the need to mark you."

"How'd you know about that?" she asked. She'd washed off his scent long before Dannon had come home.

"Because he told me. Because he's just as freaked out as I am. Someone—probably Fuckface Kian—hates me enough that he'd probably be willing to hurt you just to get to me. That's not something I'm willing to risk, Flora."

Joe's hand raised in the air like a school kid. "Yeah. I kind of second that."

"What the fuck are you two trying to get at? You want me to quit my job? Give up a career I love? Let some piece of shit scare me in to hiding? Not going to happen, so you might as well let that go."

Dannon's eyes flashed even brighter and a low growl trickled up his throat. But after a few seconds, he closed his eyes and breathed deeply. He was struggling to get his beast side under control. "Every cell in my body wants to take you in the other room and cover every inch of your body in my scent."

Ooooh. That sounded like fun. But she was still mad at him and wouldn't give him the benefit of letting him know how turned on she was by that statement right now.

"Dannon, listen," she said, lowering her voice in hopes of putting them both at ease. "I don't take risks. Last night was fucked up, but I also knew my Chief was close enough to hear and see what was going on. Nothing was going to happen to me. I know it scared you both, but I've been doing this job for a really long time. And I'm not going to stop now. You both just need to learn to trust my judgement and abilities as a cop."

Crossing the room, his hand shot up and cupped the back of her head, pulling her mouth to his. His lips were rough on hers, his fangs grazing the flesh there as his tongue plunged in to her mouth. With trembling hands, he pulled her clothes from her body, bending to help when she kicked off her shoes and struggled to get her jeans over her ankles.

The second she was fully naked, he lifted her, wrapping her legs around his waist. He freed his cock and pushed in to her slowly, a hiss pulling from between his clenched teeth. He wasn't making love to her; he was filling his primal need, he was feeding from her, he was marking her. His beast side was as desperate as he was to reassure himself that she was right there, still theirs.

Walking her across the room with her legs still wrapped around him, his cock still buried deep in her pussy, he laid on the couch with her straddling him. He growled as she rose and lowered on to him, taking him slowly. Yes. He was so close to losing control.

"Show me your beast," Flora begged, and as a little encouragement, dropped her own façade, revealing her true form to the two most important men in her life.

Dannon growled deeper, but those beautiful sharp cheekbones came forward, his eyes still blazed a bright gold, and she knew he now leaned on top of those stunning wings.

Flora cried out when Dannon thrust his hips up hard, his pubic bone hitting her clit just right. She fell over the edge moments later, taking Dannon with her as her clenching sex milked him of his orgasm. He barked out her name, pulling her down to his chest, wrapping his arms around her back and holding her there.

His breath fanned over her marks as they both struggled to catch their breath. The front door opened and closed softly. Oops. They'd forgotten Joe was still there. It wasn't lost on her, though, that he'd waited until they finished to leave. Hopefully, his feelings hadn't been hurt that they'd completely left him out of their little emotion-filled fuck.

"Flora," Dannon whispered. She pulled back to look in to his face. "I love you, too."

A slow smile spread across her face. "I know."

His smile mirrored hers now but then faltered. "I won't ask you to give up your job. But please don't ask me to stop worrying about you. If I lost you—"

"You won't, demon," she said, using her pet name for him to try to put him at ease. "I'm careful. Yeah, I was caught off guard last night, but that won't happen again."

"Feel free to carry your weapon in to any of my clubs from now on," he said, raising one brow.

She pushed up to a sitting position but stayed straddling him. "Gee, thanks. Wish I'd known you didn't mind last night," she said, but softly slapped his shoulder to ease the sting of those words. Had she known he didn't care, she wouldn't have been so damn vulnerable against four males. But, water under the bridge. They had other things to worry about now. "So you didn't catch the sedan?"

"Nope. Son of a bitch was fast. Oh, your yard is pretty fucked up, by the way."

"Yeah. Joe told me they tore through it to get away from you this morning." Assholes. It wasn't bad enough they were fucking with her life and her husband's life, but they had to go and leave divots in her beautiful grass? "Why don't you come in to the station with me today? We can talk to Jane."

Tracing a finger down Flora's face, he nodded. "Yeah. That's cool. I don't know how much it'll do, but at least they can't say we didn't mention our suspicions."

Flora climbed from Dannon and headed down the hallway. "Where you going?"

"To finish my shower. I didn't get to take one earlier because I thought I was getting ready to go on a high-speed chase." She chuckled and shook her head when his brows shot up his forehead. "You can join me, but shower only. I want to get to the station and do a little more digging in to the vamp prince."

"You really don't like vampires," he said with a chuckle as he stood from the couch and followed her down the hallway.

"Do you know any of our kind who do?" To their kind, vampires were just gloried ticks. Or mosquitos. They could eat food, of course, but survived mostly from the blood of others. And the fuckers would fry in the sun, so they preferred to keep their homes in the dark, living in basements and cellars of buildings. Didn't seem like a very attractive life to her.

"Good point."

They showered and dressed quickly and headed out. Joe was sitting on her porch when they stepped through the door. "Figured you two needed some privacy," he muttered, barely glancing up from his phone as he stood and followed them down the sidewalk.

"Why are you still here?" Flora asked, hesitating just inside of the door of Dannon's car.

Joe shrugged and shoved his phone in to his back pocket. "Talk to Jane."

Well shit. Looks like Dannon was no longer the only one who required a baby sitter.

Chapter Eight

The Chief's door was closed when the three of them entered the precinct. Almost everyone stopped what they were doing and stared at Dannon as he walked beside Flora. She just didn't know how much of it was because of who he was, what he was, or how fucking hot he was. Regardless, the lust pouring from a few of them was giving her a little extra energy as she lowered in to her computer chair.

"Will you get him a chair?" Flora asked Joe, but he was already moving toward an empty cubicle before she'd finished her sentence. And then Joe hovered. "Seriously. I think we're safe in here."

"I know."

Flora rolled her eyes and turned back to her computer, but before the screen was fully lit, Jane's door opened and she stepped out of her office. When Flora glanced up at her, she frowned and jerked her head, motioning for her to join.

Looked like whatever Jane had to say wasn't exactly good news by the deep scowl between her brows. "Come on," Flora said to Dannon and Joe.

When they were all piled in to the office, Jane told Joe, "Close the door."

She sat behind her desk and shuffled papers around as Joe shut them in and leaned against the door while Dannon and Flora sat across from her boss.

"Good to see you again, Mr. Michaels," she said, finally looking up from her desk.

"Dannon."

Jane nodded then turned her eyes to Flora. "You okay?"

With yet another eyeroll, Flora groaned. "I'm fine. I'm the same as you. I heal just as quickly as you. Oh, and just like you, I'm a cop." She was getting real tired of everyone babying her all of a sudden. At least before she was mated to Dannon, she was treated the same as the rest of the force.

"I'm not worried about your physical well-being."

Flora frowned at Jane. "Then what?"

Jane glanced up at Joe. "Guess you didn't tell her."

"What now?" Flora whined. Yeah, she was fully aware how she sounded, but once, just fucking once, she wanted a normal day with zero drama.

"Prince Kian was able to get his buddy out of jail this morning. And his father issued a warning."

"What kind of warning?" Dannon said, his voice deep, his eyes flashing gold.

Jane's eyes mimicked his, but hers glowed a pretty silver. "Apparently, Kian told his daddy that he and his buddies were targeted by you and your husband," Jane told Flora.

"What? That's insane. You were there," Flora said.

"And that's what I told him. He accused me of calling his son a liar."

Dannon leaned forward, resting his elbows on his knees. "What did you tell him?"

"I told him I was indeed calling his son a liar. And I told him if his son or any of his merry band of followers ever assaulted one of my officers again, I'd lock up the entire group of them, regardless of our standing with the vampires."

Joe snorted. "I'm sure he loved hearing that."

"I'm pretty sure I've earned a shit load of enemies, but that's their problem. They still fall under the same fucking laws as the rest of the others. If anything, I mean anything at all happens with the Prince, I want to hear about it."

"Actually, that's why I brought him in today," Flora said, then proceeded to tell Jane their suspicions.

"It makes sense," Jane said. "But unless you can get me either proof or a good reason to get a warrant to search his residence, we've got nothing. Get me something, Grumio."

Flora nodded and stood, Dannon and Joe followed her out of the office. Great. She had to somehow find a way to prove Dannon's innocence while proving the Prince's guilt, all while keeping them both alive. No pressure.

Sitting back at her desk, Flora turned the chair to look at both Joe and Dannon. "What if I accept a date with that asshole? Maybe I can—"

"No!" Dannon and Joe said in unison.

"You two are getting on my last nerve."

"This isn't some cop show, Flora. You're not offering yourself up as bait. We'll figure something else out," Joe said.

"You got a better idea?"

"No. That's why I said we'll figure something else out," Joe said.

And, just like the last few times she'd spent at her desk, she got absolutely nowhere, even with both Joe and Dannon helping. The hours flew by too quickly and it was getting dark. And she was getting frustrated. Both mentally and sexually.

"I'm ready to go," Flora said, turning off her computer and stretching her arms over her head.

"I need to stop by Roxy's Delight and Cherry Light tonight. You want to ride along, or do you want me to drop you off at home?"

"No. I need to feed. I'll come with you. Joe, I'll see you later."

"Hey," Jane called from her open door.

"Yeah?"

"I want you two to stay together. If you need to split up, call Joe or me. I'm not letting this fucker play my people any longer."

Flora didn't know if she was talking about her cops or her species—which would include Dannon in her little grouping—but it didn't matter. Jane was done playing games. Flora had the feeling she'd personally hand Kian over to the Executioner now if she thought she'd get away with it.

Flora nodded and gave her boss a two fingered wave before following Dannon out of the office and on to the street.

The drive to the first club was filled with silence. It wasn't exactly uncomfortable, but it was obvious they were both lost in their thoughts, both trying to think of a way to bring Kian down, both trying to think of a way to prove he was behind it all.

The parking lot to Roxy's Delight was packed. That was definitely good for Dannon's business, but it was also good for her. She needed to feed. And there were bound to be plenty of horny men inside to fill her with an abundance of lust.

Jim met them at the door Mattie was manning when they entered the club, the sounds of thumping music and whistling men mingling with the scents of booze, sweat, and arousal. Flora inhaled deeply and sucked a huge wave of lust in to her, filling her in one fell swoop. That would hold her over for at least the next hour.

"Could you take my wife to my table, please?" Dannon asked Mattie. Tempted to roll her eyes and protest, Flora just raised an eyebrow at Dannon and let Mattie lead her through the throng of bodies. She couldn't detect any others, but that didn't mean they weren't there. It just meant they were really good at masking their essence just like she did.

Mattie stood beside the table, his hands clasped in front of him, his eyes on the crowd while she waited for Dannon. "Hey," she yelled up to Mattie, not sure how keen his hearing was. He glanced down at her. "You can sit."

He shook his head. "I'm okay."

"Since I'm Dannon's wife, does that kind of make me your boss?" His lip quirked up at the corner and he nodded. "Okay. Then, sit. Now. Please."

His crooked smile spread, but he lowered on to the seat beside her in the booth. But he still didn't relax. He hovered just on the edge of the seat, ready to pounce at the first sign of trouble. "This is probably rude to ask, but are you a Shifter?" He nodded; just one dip of the head. "What kind?"

He glanced at her, then turned his attention back to the crowd of people. "Bear."

"What kind?"

Mattie rolled his shoulders and moved a little like she was making him uncomfortable. "Grizzly."

"Okay. That's kind of cool." He frowned and looked at her sideways but didn't say anything else. "I'm just trying to make conversation," she admitted. It was awkward having a babysitter in

92

the club when she was packing a damn silver filled nine-millimeter. "Hey. I meant to thank you for taking care of Caren for us last night." He nodded again. "You always this quiet, or is it just around me?"

This time he actually turned his head and looked down at her. "I'm not trying to hurt your feelings," he said, a slight frown drawing his blond brows together. Did he think he was hurting her feelings by not talking to her? Hey, if it got him talking so she wasn't just sitting here like an idiot, he could think that all he wanted. "You're mated to my boss."

She blinked up at him. Blinked again. "Yeah?" Now she was confused.

"We aren't like you. Shifters mate with only one. We can't force our animals to go along with sleeping with anyone else after we've chosen our person."

"You're saying your monogamous," she said. Again, with that single head dip. "I'm not asking you to sleep with me, Mattie. Just entertain me while I'm waiting for Dannon." His chivalry and loyalty to her husband was kind of sweet. Odd to her and the way her kind lived, but still sweet. "So, are you mated now?"

He shook his head. "No. Don't want to be, either."

That confused Flora after the way he'd spoken of the way his kind bonded with their mates. "Why not?"

He shook his head. Guess that was as much as she was going to get out of him for the night. Well, at least he'd talked to her this time more than a few syllables and grunts. Dannon pushed through the crowd, shaking hands with a few people, clapping a guy on the back as he passed, then finally he made his way to her table. "You ready to head out?" he asked. "Thanks, Mattie."

"All good," the big Shifter said as he stood and took his place along the edge of the room where he could see everyone at once.

"Why was he sitting?"

"Because I pulled rank and made him talk to me."

Dannon shook his head with a snort and wrapped an arm around her shoulders, guiding her through the club and out the door. The night was warm, the air stuffy and humid. She was glad she'd chosen to wear shorts today instead of her usual jeans.

"How'd you meet Mattie?" Flora asked once they were both in the car and on the road.

"I knew his dad. He called in a favor when Mattie turned eighteen and started getting in to trouble all the time. I offered him a job on the condition he kept his act together."

"He just decided to be a good boy because you offered him a job at a strip club?" Flora asked with a disbelieving look.

"Ha! No. That wasn't the only reason. He gets to manhandle assholes who get out of control, he gets to stare at tits all night, and I pay him very well. He's head of my security team for all three clubs. It took two years, but he finally pulled it together enough for me to trust him the way I do."

"Tits and money." She shook her head, but maybe for a young man, it made sense. "He said Shifters mate for life."

"So do we," Dannon said, laying his hand on her thigh once they were in the car and on the road.

"Yeah, but he said they're one hundred percent, to the death monogamous."

"Yep. Weird, right?"

Flora laughed. "Or maybe we're the weird ones."

Life with Dannon had become so easy, minus the bullshit with the missing perverts and Kian's crap. She felt like they'd been mated for years rather than a few weeks. Maybe this was the kind of connection the Shifters found and coveted. She could almost see how they'd want to be with only that one person for the rest of their lives. She knew if she had to choose only one dick for the rest of her life it would be Dannon's. But she was glad that wasn't an issue for either of them.

Cherry Light wasn't as busy as the first club. It was also smaller and in a more remote location than the other club. A few cars and motorcycles dotted the parking lot, but that was it. "Is it always this slow?"

"It's better on the weekends," he said, wrapping his hand around hers when they met in front of the hood. "Still not as busy as my other two, but it does okay."

A rock song blasted through the speakers as a woman dressed in a thong and cowgirl hat swung her hips onstage. "Do they not strip?"

"This county only allows naked breasts."

She snickered. "Breasts?" He sounded so technical and professional.

"Tits, jugs, knockers...better?" He leaned down and pressed his lips to hers before guiding her to a table in the back of the room. This place was half the size of Roxy's Delight and there were only two girls currently on stage.

The lust was muted here and Flora was already feeling the hunger. Now that she was no longer in her professional capacity, she could feed as much as she wanted. Then again, with the way the Chief had been acting lately, she could probably feed while on business hours, as well.

"You okay here for a few?" Dannon asked as she slid in to a booth.

"I could use a drink."

Dannon waved over a waitress. "Candy, this is my wife Flora. Make sure she's taken care of," he said, handing the woman a hundred-dollar bill. Her eyes widened as she smiled and hurried to the bar.

"You're ridiculous," she said, tilting her face up when he bent over the bench.

"I know. I'll be back in a few."

"The lust in here sucks," she murmured against his lips.

"I know. If you don't find someone while we're here, we'll head over to Club D when I'm done."

"Deal." She opened for him when he pressed his tongue against her lips and tasted him before he pulled away with a smile.

Once Dannon was gone, Flora turned her attention back to the tiny crowd. The waitress came back, her drink in hand. "So, you're really Dannon's wife?"

"Yep. According to our law, anyway."

"No ring?" the woman asked, looking at her finger.

"Nah. We don't need those." Something about this woman just rubbed Flora the wrong way. She'd been so sweet when Dannon had introduced them, but now she almost seemed...catty. "Candy your real name?"

She tossed her bleached blonde hair over her shoulder and shook her head. "No. Dannon said I looked good enough to eat and gave me that nickname."

Okay. Flora was not a jealous woman and didn't care who he screwed, but the thought of this bitch anywhere near her man made something green slither through her belly. What was it about Candy that made her feel so damn possessive? Not once in her entire existence had she ever felt possessive over any of the men she'd dated or slept with.

"You've known Dannon a long time?"

Again, she tossed that platinum blonde hair over her shoulder. Did the bitch need a barrette or something? "He and I go way back. Long before you ever came in to the picture." She turned her back to leave and muttered under her breath, "And long after you're gone, too." Either she didn't know Flora could hear her clearly or she wanted her to hear. When Candy turned back, her brows were raised and a smirk was plastered on her pink painted lips. "Can I get you anything else?"

Forcing a smile on her face, Flora leaned back in her seat. "Thanks for the drink. I'll let you know if you're needed again." There was a double entendre there, but Candy was either completely unaware or chose to ignore it.

As if Candy knew she'd irritated Flora, she batted her eyelashes and skipped away with a smile. Maybe she didn't exactly skip, but she sure as fuck looked light on her feet over her role in Flora's current mood.

Sucking down her drink, Flora lifted her glass to get Candy's attention. Fuck it. She'd make the bitch work. She still wasn't sure why the woman had gotten to her; hell, she'd watched her husband get sucked by the redhead at Club D. Maybe it was the way this woman treated her bond with Dannon so lightly, as if without a

96

human ceremony they couldn't truly be mated, married, together for eternity.

Or maybe Candy was jealous of Flora's relationship with Dannon and was just trying to get under her skin. It didn't matter; this little human was nothing to her and nothing to her husband.

As the night grew, a few more patrons entered the club, but it was still slow and there wasn't enough lust to feed from. They needed to go soon so she could find some relief.

Dannon raised his hand at her as he crossed the club and disappeared through a door on the right. That must have been where his office was located. And a minute later, that blonde cunt Candy followed him right in. Okay. No big deal. That was her boss. She was probably talking to him about business, her paycheck, whatever.

So why did her body rise and carry her across the floor toward that office as if it had a mind of its own?

Flora wrapped her hand around the knob and turned, pushing the door inward. Dannon sat in a chair behind his desk with his head thrown back against the seat, while Candy knelt in front of him, her blonde hair appearing and disappearing behind the desk as she bobbed her mouth on his cock. For the first time in her life, a possessive rage rushed through her system and she felt sick.

Dannon opened his eyes and looked at her, a smile lighting up his face. He thought this was like any other time for them when they were just getting what their beasts needed. But not for her. The bitch sucking off her man had not only disrespected her, but their marriage.

She had two choices: Rip the bitch away by her hair, or turn around and leave him to finish. If she caught the faintest scent of her husband on that woman...

Returning to her table, Flora was tempted to grab one of the dudes sitting around the stages and drag him in to the bathroom. No. That would be a revenge fuck and that wasn't who she was. That wasn't who they were. What she'd walked in on was completely healthy and normal for her kind, but the fact it was with that bitch was what had her heart racing. Or was it breaking? That was stupid. Someone that insignificant could never cause a riff between her and Dannon so there would be no heart break.

When Candy exited the office, her eyes immediately found Flora…and she smirked again, tossing that hair over her shoulder. Pushing from the table, Flora stalked across the room, unsure exactly of what she intended to do to the woman when she finally caught up with her.

Candy startled hard when she turned to find Flora hovering over her. Flora inhaled deeply. That mother fucker marked this bitch; covered her with his scent. It was only near her face so he'd probably just come in her mouth, but that didn't matter. At least when Flora's best friend marked her, she had enough respect for her husband to wash away his scent. It was as if Dannon had marked his waitress on purpose.

"Did you need another drink?" Candy asked, that stupid smirk still in place. Did this little human know about scent marking? Was that why she was smiling like that?

"Flora?" Dannon called out.

Turning to glance at him over her shoulder, anger blazed hot in her chest at his confused frown. Flora moved to join him, but Candy whispered soft enough for Flora's ears only. "I've always been his favorite and I always will. Why do you think he marks me every time we fuck?"

So, the little cunt knew about scent marking. Dannon was declaring to the males anywhere near Candy that she was claimed. Oh, that mother fucker was about to get an earful from her when they got in the car.

Opening her mouth to threaten the little slut, Flora snapped it shut. She was still a cop. She had to remember that. No matter what kind of trouble she might have in her personal life, she couldn't do anything to jeopardize her career.

Flora growled softly, causing Candy to take a step back, then turned her back on the tramp and joined Dannon's side.

"You ready to head over to Club D?"

Oh. She was ready alright. "Yep."

He frowned down at her, but she wasn't doing this here. She refused to make a scene and be turned into a spectacle. She was pissed. Irate. He'd declared she was his; made sure his was the only scent she carried. Yet he had no problem marking other women. How many others were there? She hadn't really spent much time around the other strippers at his club. Did they all carry his scent, as well? He didn't leave Flora's side much, so she knew he wasn't mated to any others, but that didn't mean he wasn't going around building his own personal fucking harem.

Chapter Nine

Flora was acting weird. She tensed when Dannon laid his hand on her thigh as they drove to Club D. It was probably the stress of what was going on with his case. But when he'd asked if she was okay, she'd forced a smile and said she was fine. Maybe he didn't fully understand the female species, but everyone knew fine was just the term for you're in big fucking trouble. She wouldn't tell him any more than that.

Pulling his car along the curb, he offered his keys to the valet and pressed his fingers to the small of Flora's back, leading her in to the club. The place was packed for a Tuesday night. He guided his wife to a table along the back and leaned close to her ear.

"What are you in the mood for?" he asked. Flora pulled away from him and glared. "Okay. What the fuck is going on with you tonight?"

"How many other women carry your scent?"

He frowned at her. What the hell did that mean? "Uh, you?"

"Oh, and Candy. Let's not forget her. Who else?"

Shit. When he'd tried to pull Candy away when he was ready to blow his load, she kept her mouth on him and swallowed every last drop. Of course, Flora would smell him on her. "That was an accident." He was aware of how pathetic that sounded, but he couldn't think of any other excuse at the moment. Especially not when she was looking at him like she was ready to punch him in the nuts.

"An accident," she repeated. Nodding, she pushed him from the bench and stood.

"Where are you going?"

"To feed."

"Hey!" he yelled even though he knew she could hear him if he talked normal. But the way she was moving away from him made him a little nervous, both for her safety and their damn relationship.

"What?" she said, crossing her arms over her chest.

"Can't we feed together? Here?"

"You already fed," she said, shooting him a smirk, then turned on her heel and headed deeper in to the crowd.

He tracked her progress with his eyes, even standing when she got a little far from him. Shit. Now he wished he had a few of his guys so he had a few more sets of eyes on her. Hell. Even Joe would be better than nothing.

He'd hurt her. That much was evident in the way she was intent on finding someone to feed from instead of staying with him, feeding with him, feeding from him.

Oh shit. Kian was there and he'd noticed Flora moving through the crowd. The cock sucker had his usual groupies with him, including the big fucker who'd put his hands on her last night. She didn't see them yet, but they were heading right toward her.

Pushing through the crowd, Dannon tried to get to her as quickly as possible, hoping to head the Prince off before he could rile Flora up or cause any more problems.

Flora turned her head and spotted Kian, then turned to look for Dannon. But he was already on his way. Kian approached Flora, but Dannon couldn't hear shit over the booming bass. Flora found Dannon, shook her head, then followed Kian through the tight crowd.

What the fuck?

There was no way his wife was considering feeding from Kian just to get back at him. No fucking way.

When Dannon finally found Kian's bodyguards, they were hovered around a private room and refused to budge. "Get the fuck out of my way, assholes," Dannon growled out.

"Nope. Sorry, dickhead. Your wife said she wanted some privacy."

Dannon's heart stopped. It literally stuttered in his chest and his stomach turned. No, they weren't monogamous, but he'd never thought she would sleep with not just a vampire, but his fucking enemy. Their enemy. The piece of shit was trying to take Dannon down. He was making it look like Dannon had something to do with the murders. And now she was behind the doors, letting him do…

No. He couldn't think about that. Nope. Because if he pictured Kian buried inside of his mate, he'd tear through those mother fuckers and then tear the Prince's head from his fucking shoulders. And he didn't give two shits if that started a fucking war.

When Flora had stepped away from Dannon, her sole focus was revenge. Yep, it was childish, but she was hurt. But when Kian had approached, another idea had hit her. She knew Kian could smell the anger pouring from her when he approached. Maybe she could use it to her advantage.

"Miss Grumio," Kian had greeted her. She struggled to keep from making a disgusted face at his pathetic attempt to charm her and make it look like she was interested. "I just wanted to apologize for what happened last night. My guys get a little carried away sometimes."

She shrugged but crossed her arms over her chest. "It's fine. I was being a bitch." Ugh. She'd never been a good liar, but she really had to try to make him believe every word that came from her mouth. "And call me Flora."

"You look upset. Something I can help with?"

Glancing over at where she'd left Dannon, she almost panicked when she realized he was already moving through the crowd. If he got to them before she lost her nerve, the plan would never work.

"I'm just hungry. And Dannon apparently found his own private feeder." She shrugged.

"Maybe I can help?"

Swallowing back her disgust, she smiled. "That would actually be kind of nice. I'm pissed at him and really don't want to be around him right now." It was half true.

He took her by her elbow, his touch gentle, and led her through the crowd to one of the private rooms. I can do this. I can do this. She'd never fucked a vampire, but if it would save Dannon's life and keep him out of jail, she would sacrifice her body just this once.

"Can you make sure we have some privacy?" she said to the asshole who'd hit her last night.

He smiled a cruel smile, his eyes roaming her body, and nodded.

The room was dark and empty, and the scent of sex and sweat clung to every surface. She could only imagine how brightly it would glow under a blacklight.

When Kian dipped his head to kiss her, she turned her head and offered her throat. Not smart considering he could sink his fangs in her, but she couldn't stomach the thought of his lips on hers.

And as he laid clumsy pecks along her neck, his hand cupping her tit, she realized she couldn't stomach the thought of him being inside of her either. "I want to make you feel good," she said, squeezing her eyes shut against the tears that burned the back of her eyes. Please forgive me, she screamed in her head as she pictured Dannon's face when he realized what she had done.

Reaching down, she undid Kian's pants and slid her hand in to his pants. Shockingly, he was well-endowed. For some reason, she'd pictured him having a smaller cock, maybe even a crooked one. But it was thick and engorged and had a drop of moisture at the head.

Kian moaned against her neck as she stroked him. This was the best she could offer, but she had to do something to convince Kian she didn't hold a grudge against him. If she could convince him to trust her, maybe she could get him to confess what he'd done. It was a long shot, but it was the only thing she could think of at the moment.

With her hand still in his pants, she let Kian fondle her tits, pinch her nipple through her tank top as she jacked him off. It didn't take long before he was panting and close. Tilting her head back further, she faked a moan when he squeezed her tit hard and stroked him faster. It worked. He came, his cum coating her hand and the inside of his pants. He grunted with each pump until he was spent.

Pulling her hand from his pants, she looked around for something to clean off with. Nothing. Shit. Squeezing her eyes shut, she wiped her hand on her shorts and fought the grimace when she realized she'd wreak of him until she was able to get home, shower, and change.

"I would've preferred to make love to you for our first time," Kian said, buttoning up his slacks.

Make love. Who did this dude think he was talking to? Or was that the kind of crap he spewed to every woman he fooled around with?

"I know. I was just so hungry and…well…"

"What?" he asked.

Swallowing back the bile, she looked up at him through her lashes. "I'd wondered what your cock would feel like in my hand since last night. Something about the way you were so in to me…" She shrugged. "I don't know. I just couldn't admit it in front of anyone else. You won't tell your friends, will you?" How the hell he could buy her innocence act…

"Of course not. I don't kiss and tell. What about your husband?"

She shrugged again. "Can't we just be a secret?"

His smile was wicked and he chuckled low. "You're not really in to him, are you?"

Okay. Now she could actually tell a little bit of truth. "He marked me without my permission." See? Not a lie. And she didn't have to directly answer his question. "And he scent marked another woman tonight. A human stripper."

He nodded, his face sympathetic. This dude was either a really good actor or seriously unhinged if he was buying her theatrics. "I figured he did. How could any Incubus be around that much pussy and not give him?" He held his arms out and hugged her to his chest. Wow. The dude was holding her, trying to comfort her. And all she could think about was how hard this was all going to be on Dannon when they got home.

She knew it would hurt him, but he'd hurt her. They were even. The difference was her little betrayal could possibly benefit his case.

"I should get back out there before he figures out what we're doing. Can I call you?"

His eyes widened. Yep; he was buying it. Pulling his phone out, he asked for her number. Entering it in to his phone, he called her so she could program his number. "I can't wait to hear from you."

Flora smiled at him, then turned her back on him, taking a deep breath before pulling open the door. And Dannon was right there, held back by Kian's guards.

She couldn't look him in the eye as she passed him. She didn't miss the deep inhale. He smelled Kian all over her. Hell; his spunk probably wasn't even dry on her shorts yet.

Dannon followed her out of the club, and didn't say a word to her while they waited for the valet to bring the car around. But, once they were on the road, he let loose his rage. "What the fuck did you do?" he growled softly. His low tone actually cut her worse than if he'd screamed at her.

"What I had to."

The car lurched to the side as he whipped the wheel. The seatbelt locked in place, keeping her from hitting the dash when he slammed on the brakes. "You had to fuck my fucking enemy? You had to fuck the son of a bitch trying to get me executed? At least I know you'll be taken care of when my head is taken from my body."

Flora turned in her seat. "Number one: I didn't fuck him—"

"I can smell him all over you."

"I gave him a hand job. That's not the same as, oh I don't know, coming in someone's mouth and declaring them your favorite."

"What are you talking about? Yeah; I came in her mouth. I tried to pull away and she kept her mouth on me. I never said she was my favorite."

"Nope. She was pretty forthcoming with the history between the two of you."

His mouth hung open as he stared at her wide-eyed. "You fooled around with Kian because a human stripper tried to make you jealous?"

Flora's heart raced and she was trembling. But she wasn't sure how much of it was anger and how much of it was shame of what she'd just done. There was a part of her that had done it to intentionally wound Dannon to get back at him for the thing with Candy.

"I fooled around with Kian to try to gain his trust. I want that mother fucker to tell me what he's doing. He doesn't seem all that stable. Maybe I can make him fall for me and tell me all of his secrets."

Dannon slammed his head against the headrest and closed his eyes. "Fuck," he growled out softly.

He pulled the car back on to the road and sped home, surpassing the speed limit by a lot. When they got to his house, she turned to watch him climb from his seat. He rounded the car, yanked her door open, and pulled her from her seat. She squealed when he quickly lifted her from the ground and damned near ran in to the house with her in his arms.

"What are you doing?" she said as he rushed in to the bathroom. He didn't take her clothes off as he turned on the spray and stepped under it. "Dannon, you're freaking me out."

"I can't stand his smell on you," he said, his voice too deep and guttural to pass for human.

He glanced at her and looked away, but she'd caught the shimmer of moisture there. Fuck. She'd hurt him way more than she'd intended. Finally setting her on her feet, he peeled her soaking wet clothes from her body and proceeded to wash her from head to toes, focusing a lot of attention on her thighs and hand where Kian's scent had been concentrated.

"Dannon, stop," she said, grabbing both of his hands to still him. "Look at me."

"Why him? Out of every male in this city, why Kian? Why that asshole?"

Flora inhaled deeply. "Honestly? I didn't intend to do anything with him at first. I was just walking off with him to piss you off. I wanted you to feel the way I did when I smelled you on that bitch at your club. But, when I realized I could possibly be the piece to put this big ass puzzle together, I was willing to sacrifice myself and my sanity if it meant keeping you out of the hands of the Executioner."

106

"Were you willing to sacrifice us?"

That drew her up short and her head snapped back as if he'd hit her. The words were sharp enough it felt like he'd physically struck her. "Of course not," she said barely above a whisper. Her throat felt like it was closing as emotion choked her.

"I don't care who you feed from. And I don't care how you get your needs met, but...not Kian. Never again."

"Dannon—"

"If you feel the way you say you do about me, please..." He trailed off, shaking his head slowly from side to side.

"Listen to me." She cupped his face in both hands as the water hit her back. "First of all, how can you possibly question how I feel about you? Seriously. That was a pretty shitty thing to say. And second," she inhaled deeply before continuing, "as much as me being with Kian hurts you, I'm willing to do anything to keep you alive. Even if that means being with that asshole prince. I'm sorry. I'm sorry it hurt you. I'm sorry the thought of what I might end up having to do hurts you, but I won't lose you because someone's got it out for you. The second ParaPolice have what they consider enough proof, the Executioner will be called in and you know there's nothing I can do to stop it. We can run. Right now. That's the only other option I can think of to keep any of this from going any further. Hate me if you want. Leave me if you think you need to. But I won't lose you if I can stop it."

Dannon's eyes flashed brighter than she'd ever seen a second before his wings burst from his back and his true form broke free. She had a feeling he couldn't hide it now even if he tried. Anger...maybe more...was fueling him now. His hands were rough as one gripped the back of her head, tangling in her hair while the other wrapped around her back and crushed him to her.

His lips were hard, his fangs piercing the flesh of her lips as he crashed his mouth on to hers. His kiss was full of so many emotions, so much anger, so much love, so much desperation, so much hate. Hate for Kian or hate for the fact Flora would betray him, betray his heart if it meant keeping him alive, she didn't know.

"Dannon," she whispered as his lips trailed a burning path down her jaw to her throat. Tightening his hand in her hair, he pulled her head to the side to expose more of her neck to him. His fangs grazed over her pulse point and she knew what he wanted. He was desperate to erase any part of Kian, and that meant marking her thoroughly.

Dannon released her throat and lifted her, wrapping her legs around his waist, and carried her from the bathroom, straight to his bedroom. He knelt on the bed, holding her up as he moved further up the mattress, kissing her until she felt drunk. She was feeding from just his lust—something she'd never been able to fully accomplish with any other lover.

He lowered her to the bed and clumsily fumbled with his soaked clothing, struggling to push his pants over his hips. Flora sat up and helped, shoving and peeling them off his legs as he reached up and pulled his ruined shirt over his head, his wet hair hanging loose on his shoulders, the water dripping from the ends and rolling down his beautiful chest. He was hers. All of him.

And now she couldn't seem to force herself to believe betraying him for his own good was possible. As she stared up in to his pained eyes, she realized, she'd never really wanted anyone nearly as much as she wanted him in that moment. Even if she knew she was about to be punished for her sleight.

Of course, she didn't truly mind the thought of how he was going to punish her, but she hated the reason he felt the need, the reason his beast, his inner demon felt the need to remind her she was mated, she was claimed, she was his.

The second Dannon was free of his clothes, he laid over her, covering her body from head to toe with his. The tip of his cock barely brushed against her folds as his hands burned a path from her throat to her breasts where he squeezed and kneaded first one then the other. His tongue was rough when he dropped his head and lapped at her nipple, drawing it to a tight bud before sucking it in to his mouth.

But he still didn't penetrate her. He still didn't push in to her.

"You're mine," he said, his voice so deep and guttural, more demon than man. He was far beyond any rational thought. His primal side had fully taken front seat and Flora was now just along for the ride.

"I'm yours," she agreed, wrapping her fingers in his wet hair, holding his head to her breasts.

But he was done showing them any attention. His beast needed to fully mark her, to reassure himself and prove to everyone— mainly the vampire prince—she was claimed and not to be touched without permission.

As he slammed his cock in to her, he dropped his head to the crook where her shoulder met her throat and sank his fangs in to her, taking two slow draws of her blood before pulling away, not bothering to lick the wounds to seal them.

But she didn't care. All she knew right now was pleasure, heartache, love. So many things warring for her attention and she couldn't focus on just one.

"Mine," he growled again, this time dropping his head to latch on to the swell of her tit, his fangs sinking in deeply. The sharp pain of his bite was overridden as his pumps became faster, harder, more aggressive. He didn't drink from her this time; just pulled from her and moved to the other tit, sinking his fangs in again.

He was scarring her with his bites, with his venom. Oh, she had every intention of returning the favor, but right now, this was for him, for his mental well-being, for his beast's sanity.

"I'm yours, Dannon. I'm yours," she breathed out as the first wave of orgasm bloomed, the pressure building to blinding just before exploding from her middle out, drawing his name from her lips.

He growled low, his eyes blazing bright, and he tensed, slamming in to her once more and going rigid as he filled her. But he wasn't finished. Within seconds, his cock was rock hard again and he was ready for more. Before he was finished, he covered her stomach, her tits, her ass, even her back and thighs before rolling on to his side, the glow behind his eyes finally dimming as he tried to catch his breath.

"I'd rather the Executioner take me than to have you in Kian's hands ever again."

Fuck. He wasn't going to let this go. And for the life of her, she couldn't find a good enough argument anymore. The four orgasms that turned her brain to jelly might have had a big part in it, but she had a feeling it was so much more. For the first time since her sexual awakening, she didn't want to fill her needs with anyone else. For the first time in her entire existence, she truly hoped she could find a way to feed solely from Dannon so she'd never again have to let another man inside of her.

Because, as the little holes Dannon had made in her throat and both tits slowly seeped blood before they healed over, she realized Dannon was all she needed. He might have originally marked her without permission, binding them, binding their beasts, but she couldn't think of another soul on this planet she'd rather spend eternity with than the man now staring in to her eyes with such raw emotion it broke her heart.

"Never again," she promised, rolling over and throwing her leg over his hips, straddling him.

This time, when she took him in to her, lowering slowly, she truly made love to him. Even as she gently sank her fangs in to the flesh over his pec, she could feel her heart swell. She could feel her soul sigh in contentment as if happy that her mind and heart had finally caught up.

Chapter Ten

"So, what are you going to tell the Prince?" Dannon asked the next afternoon after they'd slept well past morning. His fingers made lazy circles around her tight nipple, tempting her to drag him on top of her.

She shrugged, her shoulders touching the pillow before she relaxed again. "I'll tell him I changed my mind."

"You think that'll be enough?" Dannon said with a chuckle.

Neither of them had tucked away their wings or hidden their true forms before they'd fallen asleep tangled in each other's arms. They didn't need to. Not with each other. There was nothing more beautiful to her than her man in his Incubus form, just as he found her the most beautiful when she looked like a true Succubus.

"Does it matter? What's he going to do? Have his sycophants kidnap me and tie me down to his bed?"

Dannon's eyes flashed gold for a half second, and he grinned a feral smile. "I dare any of those fuckers to touch you again."

"Dannon, I was kidding. I do want to talk to him, though. I want to know where the hell he got that picture. I mean, seriously. Who the hell took that? And why send it to him?"

"Who all did you fuck in your bed before you bought a new comforter?"

She raised her eyebrows. "Seriously? Can you tell me every single woman you've had in this bed?"

"Yes."

"Bullshit. Go for it."

"You."

She stared at him, her heart rate kicking up. "What do you mean?"

"I've never had another woman in this bed. If I brought them home, they never made it past the couch. I'd bend them over, fuck them, then take them home or send them on their way. Every single

111

one of them knew they were here for one reason only, so I never heard any complaints."

"Any men?" she asked, cocking one brow and smiling a wicked smile at him.

"Uh, no. Why? How many women have been in your bed?"

"No matter how many times you ask, or how many times you think asking will make me reconsider my stance on it, I'm strictly one hundred percent dick." He chuckled and she playfully slapped his arm. "Okay. No women in your bed. How many in your house then, smartass?"

"Chhh…no idea."

"Exactly. I had that bedspread for about ten years. No idea when those were taken or by who. But there had to be a number when it was sent to Kian."

"I'd rather you not go see him alone," Dannon said.

"I agree. So, I was hoping maybe I could invite him to one of your clubs. That way, you're there, and if you're busy, Mattie or one of the other guys can keep an eye on Kian's buddies."

"You like Mattie," he said, no judgment or jealousy in his tone.

"Yeah. He's a good guy. And he's clearly loyal to you. Not to mention the way he stayed with Carin when we had that trouble outside your club."

"I didn't really give him a choice."

"Yeah, but he could've easily said fuck you to anything you ask. He cares about you." She shrugged. "I don't know. I know you're a dude and just as strong as I am, but I like the idea that he has your back when I'm not around with my gun."

"Awww … my little overprotective demon."

Flora squealed and squirmed away as Dannon poked at her ribs and squeezed her ass when she tried to roll away. At least his mood was better now. Being as she still needed to meet up with Kian sometime today, that mood might not last very long.

"Well, hello," Kian's voice purred over the line.

Flora crinkled her nose at her reflection as she held the phone between her shoulder and cheek. "Hey," she said.

"I didn't expect to hear from you so early." His voice sounded thick from sleep. It was only around twelve-thirty in the afternoon, so the night dweller had probably been out cold when she'd called him.

"I forgot you'd be sleeping. Want to call me later?"

"It's fine," he said, sounds of fabric rustling over the phone. "You okay?"

Frowning, Flora glanced over her shoulder. Who the hell was this guy? One second, he's more or less allowing his bodyguards to rough her up, and now he was concerned about her well-being? "Why wouldn't I be?" Her eyes narrowed as she waited for his answer.

"I figured Dannon would be pissed when he found out about us."

She opened her mouth to tell him there was no us, but snapped it shut and squeezed the bridge of her nose as a tension headache began to build behind her eyes. "Can you meet me sometime today? Tonight." Of course, it would be at night. He couldn't go in to the sun lest he turn into a walking bonfire.

"Of course. I'd be honored. Where?"

"Roxy's Delight?"

Silence. More fabric rustling as if he'd sat up and thrown the blankets away from his legs. "Why there?"

She could lie. She could tell the truth. Nope. Lie it was. "I guess I'm still a little wary of your guards. Tomas really doesn't seem to like me much."

After a few seconds of hesitation, Kian chuckled. "Yeah. He's a bit overzealous at times. He was punished after hurting you that night. I just want you to know that."

Flora turned and leaned her hip against the vanity sink and frowned at the wall. If he was telling the truth and he was being genuine last night and now, this guy didn't match up with the piece of shit she'd pegged for framing Dannon for kidnapping and murdering humans. Either he was a really good actor, or there was someone else involved.

"I appreciate that. Will you meet me?"

Kian sighed heavily in to the phone. "Yeah. Yeah. I'll meet you. What time?"

"When can you leave your house?"

"Sunset. I'll meet you out front around nine."

"How about we meet inside the doors? At least until I feel like I can trust Tomas." Which would be never. But he didn't need to know that.

Another heavy sigh blew static over the phone, but he finally agreed. After Flora ended the call, she took a quick shower, brushed her teeth and hair, and set out to find Dannon. He was at the kitchen table wearing nothing but a pair of sweats, his long hair disheveled after the several hours long fuckfest and going to sleep on it still wet. Her hair hadn't faired much better when she'd left the bed.

"Kian's meeting me at Roxy's Delight at nine tonight."

He nodded, just a dip of his head, then gestured to the mug sitting across from him with a jerk of his chin. He was awful quiet all of a sudden. Once she was seated across from him, she narrowed her eyes over her raised coffee mug. "What's up?"

"With what?"

"You look way too serious and you're being unusually quiet."

Dannon sighed, reminding Flora of Kian for a brief second. He dropped his eyes to his mug and studied its contents for too long. She shifted in her seat, uncomfortable with where this conversation might head. Her man was rarely serious.

"I had no right to tell you who you could and couldn't feed from. And I really had no right to scar your tits."

"I returned the favor," she said, trying to ease some of his anxiety.

He raised his hand as if to tell her he didn't deserve her forgiveness. "You know how I feel about Kian, but I had no right to tell you what you could and couldn't do. Period. You have to feed, same as I do, and…" He pushed his fingers through his long hair, shoving it out of his face. "If you have to…just please shower his scent off before you meet up with me."

Flora reached across the table and wrapped her hand around his. "Look at me." It took a second, but Dannon finally raised his eyes to her face. "I won't sleep with Kian. I won't feed from anyone but you anymore."

"You and I both know that's not always possible. We both work."

"Then I'll feed from Joe or others' lust. Just like you do with your club, I'll find my own source." Dannon's lip quirked up just at the corner. "I'm sure Joe wouldn't mind hooking you up, too."

Dannon snorted, and this time a real smile was present. "Trust me when I say he's tried."

Flora frowned at him. "When?" She knew her friend and coworker had a mild crush on her mate, but he hadn't told her he'd propositioned Dannon.

Shaking his head, Dannon lifted his mug again. "It's been a while back, before I even knew you existed. He used to come in to the club with a date every once in a while. I had to let him down. He's not exactly my type."

Flora just stared at Dannon. Joe had never told her he'd frequented Dannon's clubs before. He'd never mentioned he even knew who Dannon was before they started investigating him. Then again, the Fairy was a bit of a slut and he probably went anywhere tits or dicks might be easy to find.

"I don't want Kian. I hope you believe me. I don't want anyone but you, Dannon. I love you more than I ever thought possible. The night you marked me, I said something about being crazy in love when I found my mate? Maybe I didn't feel it that night, but I do now. I'm bone deep, heart pounding, soul shaking in love with you, Dannon."

His eyes softened as the slow smile spread across his lips. "I love you, too, Flora. God. I love you so much."

He stood on the bottom wrung of the stool and leaned over the table as far as he could. Flora met him halfway, tasting the coffee on his lips, reveling in his taste as he swiped his tongue in to her mouth once, twice before pulling back. He lowered back in to his chair but kept a death grip on her hand.

"Now that we got all that out of the way...Candy..."

"What about her?"

"No more. I don't care how hungry you are, no more feeding from that bitch. She did that on purpose last night to hurt me. She disrespected me, she disrespected us, she disrespected our bond."

"You're still mad because I came in her mouth?"

"Because you marked her after the way she talked to me."

"What exactly happened?"

Flora told him about how Candy treated her after he walked away; about how she tried to convince Flora that she was nothing but a whim and that Candy would always be his number one pick.

"She's ridiculous," Dannon said. "That was the first time she ever offered to feed me."

Flora's brows shot up her head. "Are you fucking serious?"

"I don't proposition my employees. I've never fucked or fooled around with any of my girls. I either feed from the lust in the room or I find a willing member of the audience. Or I used to."

"Hey. I never said you had to stop feeding from other women," she said with a chuckle. But the thought of two of their kind forming a monogamous relationship had her intrigued. Was it possible? Could they do it?

"You're sitting there wondering how long we'll last not feeding from other people, aren't you?" His smile was mischievous. "We could always make it interesting."

"Hmm," she said with a smile. "Let's hear it."

"Let's see how long we can go feeding from only each other. That includes lust. The winner chooses the other's punishment."

"Punishment?" she said, dropping her head and looking up at him with raised brows.

"I'm already picturing you with that redhead from Club D," he said, casting his eyes to the side as if he were fantasizing about the two women naked.

"Okay. Does that mean if I win, I get to see you with another man?" His mouth popped open and his eyes widened as he shook his head slowly side to side. "Oh please. How do you know you wouldn't like getting your dick sucked by another man if you never tried it?" She loved teasing him. Loved to see how much she could shock him.

"How would you know you don't like pussy if—"

"Already tried it…a few times. I prefer a big dick over fingers and tongue only any day."

"Ha!" Dannon released a surprised bark of laughter. "Damn. You're so fucking sexy."

After screwing once more, Flora headed in to the precinct while Dannon met with his accountant. Flora sat at her desk, once again going over the files of the missing pedophiles and rapists and comparing them to the men who were found dead. Literally the only things in common with the men were the facts they were all evil scumbags and had been to Dannon's club at some point. Seriously looked bad to anyone who didn't know her mate, but she knew better. He might despise the disgusting human monsters, but he was no murderer.

"What's up?" Joe said from behind her. The sneaky Fairy had managed to walk up on her and sit on the corner of her desk without hearing him approach. She started hard and whipped her head around. "Damn. Jumpy much?" he said, playfully pushing her shoulder.

"How long have you been sitting there, you freaking creeper?"

"I literally just sat down."

"You scared the shit out of me." She turned back to her computer screen and stared at the pictures and info she'd been staring at since the day she'd been assigned to Dannon's case. "What are you doing tonight?" she asked, not bothering to see if he was still behind her.

"Not a damn thing. Why? Got plans?"

"I'm meeting Dannon and the vamp Prince at Roxy's Delight. Want to join?"

"Hell yeah. This sounds like all kinds of fun drama. Why the hell are you meeting the Prince? I thought you hated him."

"I do. But…you know how he sent that picture of me fucking someone to Dannon's phone?"

"Uh, no. When did this happen? Who were you screwing?"

"About a week ago, and I have no idea. It had to have been before Dannon crashed in to my life because I hadn't changed the bedspread yet. But, it definitely wasn't Kian because I've never

117

fucked him. So, I want to know who sent it to him and why the hell they would do that."

"You think he'll tell you?"

Flora turned her chair to look up at Joe. "You have to promise me not to laugh."

"I can't promise that. I have no idea what you're going to say."

"At least promise not to tell anyone else."

"That, I can do." He held up his hand like a boy scout.

"I kind of gave Kian a hand job last night and now he thinks we're…friendly."

"You did not," Joe said, his eyes as wide as his smile.

"Yeah. I was pissed at Dannon for marking this whore from his club—"

"What? What whore? Woman, I have no idea what the hell you're talking about."

"Long story. But I was mad at him for that and planned on just flirting with Kian to make him jealous. But then he started acting all affectionate and mushy, like maybe he wasn't really chasing after me just to piss Dannon off like I'd thought. So, I jacked him off in hopes of getting him on my side and convincing him to tell me how he's involved in Dannon's case."

"You really think it's him?"

"I did. But now, I don't know. You should've heard him on the phone this afternoon. He was talking to me like we were close or something. And he said he punished that big dude for hitting me. I'm not saying I believe him, but that's what he said."

"Holy shit! You've got to give me more information than that. How big is the Prince's dick? How long did he last? Did he touch you? More importantly, how did Dannon react after?"

Flora shook her head and rolled her eyes. "You know, I'm the one who's supposed to think about sex all the time."

"Oh please. Like your kind has that market cornered. Fae and Pixies are just as amorous."

"I don't think what either of us do can be considered amorous," she teased, turning back to her computer. But then images

118

of Dannon lying beneath her last night as she rode him slowly ran through her head. Yeah; that was definitely romantic. It was the first time she'd ever made love to someone. Dannon was giving her all kinds of firsts lately.

"Well? Answers, please."

"Yes; his dick is nice. He lasted about five minutes, but I was trying to get him off quickly. And Dannon was crushed." Her heart stuttered at the memory of his eyes when she'd walked out of the room.

"Really?" Joe asked low, all teasing out of his voice. "He didn't hurt you, did he?"

"What? No. Of course not. He marked the shit out of me, but I wouldn't say what he did to me last night could be considered painful." Flora turned around again and did a double take. "You seriously look worried, Joe." She couldn't help the laugh. "I'm a fucking cop. I wish you and Dannon would remember that. Oh, and I'm the same fucking species he is, so I'm just as strong and fast. Stop worrying. Please."

"I can't help it. First, with that asshole guard of Kian's, and then you tell me your man punished you for letting Kian mark you…you're my girl. I'm supposed to look after you."

She opened her mouth to remind him that she was not, indeed, his girl. Maybe his friend, even his best friend as he'd called her, but not his girl. But he interrupted her. "So, I'm invited to the club tonight?"

"That reminds me," she said, the smile back on her face. "You want to tell me why you never mentioned frequenting Dannon's club and trying to fuck him?"

The grin on Joe's face faltered, but he blinked a few times and the happy-go-lucky Fairy was back. "Oh please. It was twice, and that was a while ago. And I only asked him if he wanted a blow job one time. He makes it sound like I was stalking him or something."

"No he didn't," Flora said, turning back to her computer again. "We were talking about how I still have you to feed from when he's not around and I jokingly reminded him you'd probably be game to helping him out, too."

Silence. Flora looked over her shoulder and Joe was staring at her wide-eyed, his lips parted a little. "What did he say to that?"

"Wow. You really do have a crush on my mate." She turned away and shook her head. It was one thing to think Dannon was hot. He was. Like, smoking, bad boy biker, hair in the wind hot. But it was a totally different thing to constantly think there was a chance at having sex with her husband. Not that she cared who he fucked, but Joe was going a little overboard. "He's not bi, Joe. Sorry to burst your bubble. What? I'm not enough for you?"

Another beat of silence and Joe forced out a huff of laughter. "You know you're all I need, baby girl. My dream woman."

"Oh gag. Don't you have some work to do or something?"

Joe chuckled as he left her cubicle and sauntered to his own desk. He was acting so weird since the almost attack at the club. It was normal to feel a little protective about your friends, but he was acting…possessive. Or maybe she was just reading in to things because she was so on edge with everything going on.

"Grumio," the Chief called from her office.

Flora groaned softly, pushed away from her desk, and headed to where Jane leaned against her doorway with her arms crossed under her breasts. She jerked her head, motioning Flora inside. Once both women were inside, Jane closed the door and rounded her desk, her eyes on Flora as she lowered in to her expensive looking chair.

"Any chance you've found anything else?" Jane asked.

Flora narrowed her eyes at her boss. There was something about the way Jane was looking at her that made her nervous. "Not yet. I'm meeting with the Prince at nine. Why?" Jane continued to watch Flora. "They found another of the missing men." Jane nodded slowly. "Where? When?"

"This afternoon. He was decomposed enough to prevent any identification by face alone. But he had a tattoo on his left bicep. His identity was confirmed by a family member an hour ago."

"So why am I just now hearing this?"

"Where's Dannon?"

Flora's brows dropped instantly. "Why?"

"Where's Dannon Michaels?"

"Are you planning to arrest him?" Flora rested her back against the seat and crossed her arms over her chest. If Jane thought for one second she was going to hand her mate over to be executed she was fucking nuts.

Jane leaned forward, her elbows resting on her desk top. "There's another missing male. Human. Another registered sex offender."

"Another pedophile," Flora said, rather than ask. She already knew the answer.

"Another pedophile. Where was Dannon Michaels at approximately two this morning?"

"With me."

"And where was that?" Jane asked, clasping her hands in front of her. She hated when Jane went all professional on her. How many times had she been in here when someone was under the desk giving the woman head? And now she wanted to pretend to be her superior?

"We were at his house. And trust me when I say I can confirm that he at no point left through the morning until we split up around noon today. He went to his accountant's, which I'm sure can be confirmed. Why is he being implicated in this man's disappearance?"

"Because he'd been seen at Dannon's club."

"So has Joe. So have you and Carin. Does that mean one of the two of you could be the perp?"

"Flora, be fucking serious. I'm trying real hard to keep your mate alive. I need you to stick to that man like glue. Do not let him leave your sight. You're out of this office until we can find out who's responsible. Joe can back you up if you need to leave for whatever reason. I don't want a gap of one minute."

"Fine. Done. Anything else?"

"Get me fucking proof that the Prince is involved. I want this over. I want these men found. And I want the press off my fucking back," Jane said, finally sitting back in her chair.

"Are we done?"

"Yeah. We're done."

Flora stood and opened the door. She stopped and looked at her boss over her shoulder. "I'm going to be at Roxy's Delight tonight to meet with Prince Kian. Joe might be coming, too. Feel free to stop by."

"Wasn't aware I needed your permission."

Rolling her eyes, Flora stepped out of Jane's office. "You know what I meant."

Great. Another missing fucking pedophile. And of course, he'd been by one of Dannon's clubs. But that narrowed down nothing. A lot of men went to titty bars every day. Just because he'd been to one of Dannon's didn't mean squat.

"What's wrong now?" Joe whispered as Flora passed.

"Another missing pervert."

"Greeeat," Joe drawled out.

The next few hours were spent going over everything she could find about the new case and anything she could find on Prince Kian and his family. There had to be a connection. Something to tie Kian to the men.

With a dull throb behind her eyes, Flora was relieved when eight thirty rolled around. Time to head out to see her man.

"I thought I told you to glue yourself to Dannon's hip," Jane said as she stepped next to Flora's desk.

"He's at work with plenty of witnesses. I was trying to find some correlation between the Prince and the new guy."

"Nothing," Jane said, opening a mirror and checking her lipstick.

"Nothing," Flora repeated. "I take it you're coming to the club."

"Yep. You guessed right. I'm driving, though. I need to duck out a little early tonight."

Joe was already by the door, his keys in hand when the two women were ready to leave. Joe and Flora rode together since she'd be riding home with her mate. Jane followed closely, her headlights casting the interior of Joe's car in light. "You think she can follow any closer," Joe grumbled as he adjusted his mirrors to get the bright light out of his eyes.

The parking lot was packed at the club. Good. Good for Dannon's business and good that he had a lot of people to vouch for his whereabouts since Flora failed to jump and run to his side the second she was done with her meeting with Jane.

Joe made Flora wait while they waited for Jane to catch up. "That way, if any of the Prince's goons get any ideas, there are three cops to fuck him up."

Flora was doing so much eye rolling, it was a surprise they didn't get stuck in the back of her head. Finally, they were through the door and the first thing Flora did was seek out her mate. There. Talking to the Prince who was sitting at a VIP table across from him. Great. No way this could go badly.

Chapter Eleven

It took everything in Dannon's power not to lunge across the table and rip the vamp's fucking throat out. As the arrogant prick sat there rattling on about who fucking knew what, all Dannon could picture was his woman's hands on him. At least she hadn't let the asshole fuck her.

As he clenched his fists on his thighs, he glanced up and caught the most beautiful blonde in the world walking his way. Every time he saw her it was as if he'd forgotten how gorgeous she was. And she was his. Hell; she'd even made it sound like she'd try for monogamy for him. Ha. Like that shit would ever happen for creatures like them. Oh, but he planned on holding out as long as possible so he'd be the one doling out the punishment at the end of their little bet.

Kian must've realized Dannon had tuned him out and turned to see what he was looking at. The urge to gouge out the asshole's eyes was strong, but he restrained himself. Barely.

"Hi," Flora said when she approached, Joe and their boss right behind her. Both of the other cops were already surveying the room for their next conquest. They'd be better off going to Club D where they'd be guaranteed to find a playmate or two.

"What's up?" Dannon said, standing and offering Joe his hand. The man's grip was tight and something flashed in his eyes. Probably the same fucking hate for the man sitting across from him that Dannon had. "Want to sit?"

"Nah. I want to check out the merchandise. Want to join me, Jane?" She smiled and slipped her hand through the crook of Joe's arm. He glanced back once as he walked away, raising his brows at Flora as if to ask if she was okay.

Dannon liked that he looked after Flora, but he also needed to remember her mate was sitting right there. Not a fucking chance in the world he'd let anything happen to her.

Flora sidled around the table and slid in to the booth directly next to Dannon. Kian frowned as she leaned over and pressed her lips to his. Dannon couldn't help himself; he wrapped his hands in her hair to hold her there a moment longer, swiping his tongue past her lips a few times just to taste her, and to fuck with Kian.

When Flora pulled away, her eyes glowed a faint white behind her irises. So beautiful. How he wished she could walk around in her Succubus form all day, every day. But he got it. He had to hide what he was, too.

"Can you give us a second?" she whispered. Her eyes still held that faint glow, but her brows were pulled low.

He wanted to tell her no. That he'd rather sit right there and hear every word the fucker had to say to her. He wanted to turn to Kian and tell him to go to hell. He wanted to kill the bastard for thinking he had the right to touch his mate after trying to frame him for murder. Instead of doing any of those things, he lifted Flora's hand and ghosted a kiss across her knuckles. "Let me know if you need me."

She nodded and gave him a small smile, squeezing his thigh under the table before he could scoot away and leave her alone with the man who might just be responsible for everything going wrong in his life. Then again, maybe he should thank the Prince. If he hadn't sent those pics to the police, Flora would've never come crashing in to his life. He might not live another month, but at least he found happiness and love while he was on this planet.

Dannon melted in to the crowd, his eyes on his mate as she leaned forward and said something to Kian. Her brows were furrowed, her lips set in a grim line as he answered. Looking up, he made sure he had Mattie's attention before gesturing toward Flora with a brief nod of his head. Mattie nodded back and slowly worked his way through the crowd until he was a couple of yards away. Kian might not realize he was being stalked by a Shifter, but Flora was fully aware she had plenty of backup if she needed it.

No way would he let the fuckers who stood off to the side, hawk eyeing her as if she would hurt their precious king-to-be, get anywhere near his woman. There would be a lot of blood on the floors of his club if one of them even moved in her direction. After scenting Kian on his mate, his demon was a little blood thirsty. What better way to settle his demon than to spill the blood of the fucker who'd bruised her face?

"Can I assume last night was a one-time thing?" Kian asked. Hurt flashed through his eyes before he replaced it with his usual arrogant mask. Whatever. She couldn't let his cracked ego get in the way of finding evidence he had a hand in framing her man.

"Yeah. Sorry. But I appreciate you helping me feed."

"Honey, I'd feed you every night if you let me. You could reign beside me as Queen someday and not have to worry about chasing after assholes in the middle of the night."

For a second, the blue sedan flashed through Flora's head. But she hadn't been the one chasing it. He was just speaking in general, not actually giving anything away...yet.

"Kian..." She inhaled deeply, trying to arrange her thoughts before she blew everything. "You can seriously buy any woman you want. You're royalty; surely women throw themselves at you. Why me? Is it to get to Dannon? Do you have some kind of problem with him?" Now she wished she'd thought to bring something along to record their conversation. Even if he outright confessed everything to her right here and now, it'd be her word against his since she hadn't Mirandized him. Yes; even the ParaPolice had to read Miranda rights.

"I don't want a woman who wants me for my money. And no, my attraction to you has nothing to do with your boyfriend. I'd still want you even if he wasn't in the picture." That sounded almost like a threat. A little. Or maybe she was just grasping for straws. "You're beautiful, you're strong and smart, and you're sexy as hell. What's not to like? Oh, and you carry a gun. Between your own essence and that silver loaded weapon, I'd never have to worry about my Princess getting hurt."

"I'm not yours, Kian."

"Not yet. But I won't give up."

"Yeah; you really need to." Flora squeezed the bridge of her nose. What was it about these men and causing her constant tension headaches? It was like her only stress in life anymore had to do with guys. "Who sent you the picture?" she asked, dropping her hand from her face.

His brows pulled together. "Which picture?"

"The one you sent Dannon, Kian. Don't play dumb."

"No. I literally mean which picture." He pulled his phone out and opened his picture folder. In it were at least a dozen pics of her in various states of undress, all during times she was fucking or feeding.

"What the fuck?" she whispered, yanking the phone from his hand. One of his guards took a step in her direction. "Yeah. I dare you, big boy. If I don't put a silver bullet between your eyes, the half dozen men watching you will rip your head from your shoulders. Back the fuck up."

Kian raised his hand and shooed Tomas away. Why the hell did he always have to bring that asshole around?

As Flora swiped through the pics, every single one of them was from her house, every single one of them showing her bedspread. Like she'd told Dannon, there was no way she could narrow down how many men had been through her house in the time she'd had that old bedspread. At least it wasn't anyone recent. That much was evident by the fact not a single one of them showed the comforter she'd purchased a few months back. That ruled out a few people, but that wasn't much.

"Who sent these to you, Kian?" she asked, finally peeling her eyes from her naked body splayed out on the phone's screen. What a feeling of utter violation.

He shrugged. "Don't know. They were sent to my private messaging on one of my social networks. But it's a fake profile. Tried to have one of my guys track it down…you know, to see if he had anymore." He winked, but quickly wiped the smile from his face when he realized she wasn't in the least bit amused at having her privacy invaded. "Anyway, no. It's not a real profile. No phone number, no contact info, and no pic. Sorry, Princess."

"Stop calling me that," she said absent-mindedly, her eyes going back to the screen. The pics didn't show the male; didn't show any part of his body. Just Flora, eyes closed, mouth open in the middle of what appeared to be a good time. "Please erase these," she said, raising her eyes to his.

"What? Why would I want to do that? If this is the closest I'll ever get to seeing you make that face, I want to savor them."

"Are you just trying to hurt me, Kian? Are you trying to hurt Dannon?"

His brows pulled together and he sat back in his chair. "I already told you, I don't care one way or the other about your boyfriend. I just want you. You can still keep him in your life. I know you need to feed a lot and I sleep through the day. But I want you. I'd never hurt you on purpose."

"Then please delete the pictures," she whispered, hoping his hearing was as acute as hers.

His face went neutral as he stared at her. "If I do that, can I have at least one night with you?"

"No."

Kian crossed his arms over his chest and looked around the room. She didn't know if he was thinking, biding time, or checking to see where Dannon and his men were. When he looked back at her, he nodded once. "Fine."

None of this was adding up. She'd been dead set on Kian being the suspect. She just knew he was the one who'd sent the pictures to the cops in hopes of implicating Dannon in the disappearances and murders. But this guy, the one sitting across from her pouting because she wouldn't let him keep some nudie pics of her, wasn't adding up to the image she'd built in her head. He'd said she could still keep Dannon if she'd just give him a chance and let him make her a Princess. If he was the one trying to get Dannon killed, he'd never agree to her having her mate in her life. He'd do everything in his power to separate them. Wouldn't he?

"Did you send some pictures to my boss?"

A confused frown marred his handsome face. "Why would I send naked pictures of you to your boss? I might be infatuated with you, but I'm not cruel and I'm not some crazy stalker."

"Not naked pictures of me. Did you send pics of Dannon to my boss?"

"No one sent me naked pictures of him and I really don't care to see them."

Either Kian was a damn good liar or he really didn't know what she was talking about. Fuck. If he wasn't the one behind all this bullshit, she was back to square one.

"You're not the asshole you try to pretend to be, are you?" she asked, narrowing her eyes at him.

Kian leaned forward, a small smile pulling up the corners of his lips. "Let's just keep that a secret between us."

If Kian had nothing to do with it, maybe it was the person sending him pics of her. But that, too, was a dead end according to the prince. Nah. She wasn't going to just leave that kind of information hanging. They had their own cyber people in her precinct and there had to be some kind of IP address or something she could follow.

"Do you still have that profile?"

"On my social page?" Kian asked, bringing his phone to life again.

"Yeah. Can you send it to me?"

"Uhhh…" He frowned down at the page. "I would, but it's currently unavailable?"

"What?" Again, Flora reached across the table and yanked the phone from Kian's hand. "Son of a bitch." Everything was gone. Even the pics had been deleted. How? Wait… "Did you take screen shots of all of those pics?"

His smile was mildly sheepish. "Well, yeah. I wanted to make sure I had them."

"Did you anticipate this douche deleting his account?"

"Flora, it was obviously a fake account. I wasn't taking the chances of losing all of these."

"Delete them, Kian," she growled out as she passed his phone back over the table.

He held his hands up in surrender, but she had a feeling the prince would keep at least one of them. Whatever. Let him have his little fantasy pic. She had bigger issues to worry about.

With a forced smile and a nod, Flora stood. "Thanks for..." Shit. He hadn't really done anything. "Just thanks."

"Let me know if you reconsider my offer. You'd be a beautiful Queen."

She shook her head, raised a hand over her shoulder as she walked away, and sought out Jane. She stood with Joe and Dannon, their heads close as they talked. "Hey," she said as she approached.

Everyone looked up. Dannon pulled her close to his side as if he had to have her near him. "What did the jackass have to say? Did he confess?" he asked with a smirk.

"Actually, I think I pegged him all wrong?"

"You pegged him?" Joe said with a shit eating grin.

Dannon growled low.

"Really, dude? No; I didn't peg him," she said with yet another fucking roll of her eyes. These men were going to give her a damn aneurism. "First of all, he had about a dozen pics of me. All taken at my house but at least a few months back before the new comforter, just like the pic he sent to you. And he seemed genuinely confused when I asked him about sending pics of you to the precinct."

"He could be lying," Dannon said, looking over her shoulder in the direction of where she'd left Kian sitting at the table.

"I guess he could be, but then he'd be a really fucking good actor. He thought I meant he had naked pictures of you."

Dannon's eyes dropped to her face and he frowned. "He better not."

"Oh, but the fact he's got a bunch of me in some very delicate situations is okay."

"Didn't say that," Dannon growled, his eyes flashing bright.

"Might want to calm down a little unless you want to scare all your customers."

"Where did he get the pics of you? Did he say?" Joe asked, leaning against the bar.

Flora shook her head. "They were sent from a fake social media page that has since been deleted. Is there a way to find the IP address even if it's been deleted?" Flora asked Jane.

"I don't know. I'll ask around. We'll need access to the prince's account. If I get a definitive answer, I'll ask for a warrant."

"He was pretty forthcoming when I was asking. Didn't say a word when I took his phone. He might offer up the info without a warrant, but yeah, get one just in case."

"If it's not fucking Kian, then who the fuck is it?" Dannon said, his voice deep and growly. He was pissed; she wasn't sure how much of it was from the ongoing case against him and how much of it was because the prince had naked pictures of Flora. But the anger wouldn't do shit right now. They had to keep their heads straight and try to figure out a different angle.

"What are the chances whoever is doing this is an ex-lover or something? Maybe even a disgruntled employee. Did you fire anyone within the last year?"

Dannon's head wagged slowly side to side. "No. I've had people move on to other jobs, but no firing. I'm careful about who I hire."

Candy flashed through her mind. "What if it's someone with a crush on you? Did you turn anyone down recently?"

"Other than Joe?" Dannon teased, raising one brow at Joe.

"Oh, ha ha," Joe said, lifting his beer from the bar top and taking a long pull.

"Candy made it out like you two were long time lovers but you said that night was your first time. Had you turned her down in the past?"

"I seriously don't think that tiny wisp of a woman could overpower all those men. And no, I didn't reject her. She'd never offered until that night."

"Fuck," Flora muttered.

"We're running out of time, Flora. The DA wants to take this to trial within a few months. If I can't find something concrete to fully exonerate Dannon, I'll have no choice."

"You said yourself another male went missing last night. We were together all night. There were witnesses at the club, and you'll just have to take my word for the rest of the evening and in to the morning."

"I believe you. I do. But my hands are tied. I like you, both of you, but I won't risk my job or my head to protect your mate," Jane said, setting her beer on the bar. "I'm out of here. Stick together. Call me if you figure anything out."

Once Jane was gone, the night seemed to just fly by. And Flora was getting hungry and frustrated. "You ready to head out?" Flora asked Dannon, leaning close to his side.

"Yeah."

"I'm going to use the bathroom and then we'll head out."

"Why are you guys leaving so early?" Joe whined.

"It's almost four in the morning. It's not early. Go find someone to play with and I'll talk to you later," Flora said, waving at him over her shoulder as she pushed through the crowd.

The line to the bathroom wasn't bad, but it didn't help when she knew at least one stall was taken up by someone fucking. "Come on," she yelled. "Just do it on the sink like a normal couple." She snickered to herself. Humans didn't normally bang in public. It might be normal to her to be bent over anywhere she could, but humans still preferred at least a small modicum of privacy.

Eventually, she was able to get in to a stall and then stood over the sink washing her hands. When she raised her eyes to check her reflection, Joe was standing behind her. "Hey," she said, grabbing a towel and drying her hands. "What are you—"

As she turned around, Joe ambushed her, his mouth slamming on to hers, his hand frenzied as it moved up her shirt to cup one of her tits. There were a few giggles from behind her, but Flora ignored them. With a hard push, Flora pushed Joe away. "What are you doing?"

"Fucking you. What does it look like?"

Flora looked over his shoulder at the women watching him. It was no secret to those who knew Flora and Joe that they hooked up on the regular. It was also no secret to anyone who knew what she

132

was that fucking all the time was healthy and normal for her kind. But not once in all the time Flora had known Joe had he tried to take her in front of humans.

"Not tonight, Joe," she said, pushing past him. He wrapped his hand around her bicep and pulled her to a stop as a couple of women made pained sounds at her rejection. "What the fuck are you doing?"

"Ever since you let him mark you, you've been pushing me away. What's going on?"

Flora yanked her arm from his grasp and frowned up into his face. "We just fucked a couple of days ago, Joe. How is that pushing you away?"

"I never see you anymore. You're always buried so far up his ass, it's sick. And you're willing to go down in flames with him, whether he's guilty or not."

"You know damn well he's not," Flora said, pushing him out of the way and leaving him with all those women in the bathroom.

"Hey!" he called after her as she hurried to Dannon's side. The second Dannon saw her face, his eyes flashed bright and Mattie moved closer. Flora shook her head slightly, calling them both off. Joe, she could handle. "I want to talk to you."

"Joe, go home. You're drunk. Call a cab or an uber or something and sleep it off. I'll call you in the morning."

His eyes narrowed to angry slits and moved from her to Dannon and back. "Fine."

Flora backed away, not willing to give him her back when he was acting like this. She'd never seen this side of him. She'd also never seen him drunk. Maybe he was one of those men who got aggressive with too much alcohol. If that was the case, tonight was the last time she'd go drinking with him. She really didn't like the guy glaring at her as Dannon escorted her out with a hand on the small of her back.

Mattie stepped behind them and followed them out, covering their backs. Mattie didn't know Joe was no real threat, but she appreciated the extra eyes.

Turning back once more before stepping out in to the humid early morning, Flora tilted her head at the way Joe was watching her.

Something was going on with him lately and she decided right then to find out immediately. If his personal problems ended up somehow affecting Dannon's life, she'd kill her friend herself.

Chapter Twelve

"What was that about?" Dannon asked Flora once they were in the car and on the road.

Flora leaned her head against the seat and rolled it to look up at Dannon. "I have no idea. He was in the bathroom and was trying to get me to have sex. We've never done it in public. I'm not really in to that. At least not in front of so many humans. I don't know why he suddenly thought it was a good idea."

"He looked pissed."

"I know. You should've seen him when I told him no."

A soft growl trickled up Dannon's chest. "What did he do?"

"Ugh!" Flora groaned out. "I'm fine, Dannon. He didn't hurt me. Thanks for wanting to take care of me, but I can easily whoop Joe's ass and you know it."

A proud smile pulled the corners of Dannon's lips up. "My little badass demon."

"That's better," she said, pulling his hand from the gear shifter and resting it on her thigh.

"So, you didn't feed from Joe?" Dannon asked after a few moments of silence.

Flora giggled. "Nope. Sorry. You still didn't win."

That desire to only feed from Dannon was still there; some deep-rooted need to be the only one his beast needed overriding just about everything else. She'd never experienced anything like it, but she liked it. And was severely confused by it.

"Have you wanted to feed since we split up this afternoon?" she asked, not really ready to admit how she was feeling yet. She wouldn't force him to fill his needs solely with her. It wasn't who or what they were. Just because she was feeling all sentimental and mushy didn't mean he was feeling it, too.

"Not really. I mean, I'm hungry, but..." He shrugged, his hand sliding up her thigh a little. "I don't know. No one was tempting enough to lose our bet."

He was so full of shit. Bet or no, he was in this, too. He felt that strange need she did. He just didn't want to say it. Or maybe he felt the way she did and wouldn't stifle her natural and bone deep urges. They were at a standstill because neither would admit what was going on in their hearts.

"Didn't you feed from the lust tonight?" Flora asked, twining her fingers through his just to feel his warmth.

Again, with that shrug. "Just enough to keep my energy up. I wasn't sure how Kian was going to react to your rejection. And, yes, I'm fully aware you're a badass, but there were four of them again. I didn't want a repeat of last time."

"I'm still not sure Kian is behind all this shit. From what I learned tonight, it just doesn't fit. That doesn't mean that fuckface Tomas or one of the other guards isn't fucking with you, but I don't think Kian has the slightest idea of what's going on."

"Not the best leader," Dannon muttered low.

He really did not like the Prince. Even after Flora had told him she didn't think the vamp was behind the trouble lying on Dannon's doorstep, he still held some kind of grudge. Maybe it was because the prince was after what Dannon believed was his, or maybe it was deeper rooted. Something that had been going on long before Flora had come in to his life. It didn't matter. They now had to come up with another suspect. Time was quickly running out before the powers-that-be dragged Dannon in to court to prove he was the bad guy. And then straight out back and in to the hands of the Executioner. Not as long as there was breath in her lungs.

They went to Flora's house tonight. She needed the quiet and solitude Dannon's suburbs just couldn't offer. She needed to think, and when she focused on the sound of every car passing, it was hard to work anything through her head. She felt exposed and paranoid at Dannon's. Here? Here is where she could be herself, where neither of them had to hide their wings or force their inner beasts deep in the dark recesses of their minds.

Tossing her keys on to the table near the door, Flora shuffled across the living room and dropped heavily on to the couch with a soft oomph. "I'm so damn tired," she said as Dannon lowered beside her, his hair fanning over his shoulders.

"Yeah," he said, lifting his arm so she could nuzzle against his side. "It's been a long day."

"It's been a long month," she muttered, resting a hand on his chest as she rested her head against his shoulder. "When all this is over, I want a vacation. Like, a real one. Away from here. Somewhere we don't have to use so much fucking energy hiding ourselves from humans. Is there such a place?"

He chuckled, the sound vibrating through his chest and warming her. Her need, her hunger reared its head at the masculine sound he emitted and the way he lazily stroked his fingers against her scalp, relaxing her and turning her on. Then again, Dannon didn't have to do much to get her revved and ready for him. Just being around him made her throb between her thighs.

Neither of them had truly fed since this morning. And she was starving and wanted what her man had to offer.

Dipping out from under Dannon's arms, she dropped to her knees in front of him and kept her eyes on his face as she undid his belt, snapped the button on his jeans, then slowly unzipped his pants. A sexy quirk of his lips was her only answer as she reached in and freed his already hard cock. Yep. She had the same effect on him that he had on her. They were perfect together.

Moistening her lips with a swipe of her tongue, Flora lowered her head and teased the head of his cock, pressing soft kisses around the flared head. Dannon moaned softly, almost a whisper, and dropped his head back against the couch.

Fuck, she loved that sound. And she wanted to hear more of it. No. She needed to hear more of it. She loved the fact she was the one feeding him. That she was the only one who got to hear the sounds of his pleasure today. More and more, a monogamous, or at least partly monogamous, relationship was sounding pretty fucking good to her.

Slipping her lips over his hard cock, Flora used her tongue to add more pressure, slowly dropping her head until she had as much as she could in her mouth. He was a little too large for her to take all of him, so she used her hand to bridge the gap her lips left.

"Fuck," Dannon whispered, his hand landing on the back of her head and his fingers tangling in her blonde hair.

She smiled around his cock as she raised her head. With both hands, she hooked the sides of his jeans and tugged. Dannon raised his ass as she jerked and pulled his pants down to his knees, giving her better access to all of him.

With one hand wrapped around the base of his cock, Flora used the other to cup and fondle his balls, reveling in the way his breath hitched and sped up. She knew what her man liked, and knew how to make him beg for more.

His hand tightened in her hair and he pushed her head a little faster, showing her what he wanted, showing her how fast he wanted. Mmmm. She loved him like this.

"Flora," he moaned as he balls tightened in her grip. "Stop. I want to fuck you, but I'm going to come if you keep that up."

Oh, how she wanted to taste him on her tongue. She knew that, even if he finished in her mouth, he'd be ready for another round within minutes. But she wanted him inside of her, now.

Pulling her mouth from his dick, Flora stood and undressed for him, taking her time as if she were unwrapping a gift for his eyes only. Finally naked, she straddled his hips, hovering just above his cock jutting up between his thighs.

As she slowly lowered on to him, Dannon's eyes closed, his lips parting on a soft moan, just as he had when she'd teased him with her tongue. The face she'd memorized. The one she'd grown to love was tense with restrained lust. He was trying to hold out for her, trying to make sure she went before he finished. Not that she'd let him get away without giving her what she needed.

"Flora," he whispered, his lids lifting, those beautiful brown eyes boring in to hers. With just the gaze she could feel everything he felt. She could feel his love, his devotion, his utter surrender to her. The feeling was beyond mutual.

"I love you," she whispered, riding him slowly, her hips make gentle circles as she rose and lowered.

"I love you, too," he whispered back, wrapping a hand in her hair and pulling her to his mouth.

His lips were soft as they plucked at hers, just sweet nips of her lips, a swipe of his tongue in to her mouth before going back to worshiping her lips. With his hand still in her hair, he tilted her head back, angling her jaw for better access. His lips and tongue worked the sensitive flesh along her jawline, just behind her ear, before finally landing over her pulse where he teased it with his tongue. Lowering further, she felt his fangs graze the flesh at the crook of her neck and shoulder and knew what he wanted. Tilting her head further to the side, she gave him room to take what he wanted, what he needed, what his beast required of its mate.

On the floor, in the pocket of her jeans, Flora's phone chimed, but she didn't care if someone was warning her of a meteor headed for her house. She was lost in this moment with her man, her mate, her husband for eternity. Let the meteor crash on top of their heads, as long as she didn't have to stop making love to Dannon.

Dannon's breathing was coming in shallow pants now. He was close, but so was she. His fangs gently slid in to her flesh and Flora cried out as the euphoria of his venom rushed through her system like the greatest high.

"Yes," she breathed out as she increased her tempo, Dannon's hips rising to meet her, thrusting in to her, pushing his cock deeper and shoving her right over the edge. The heat exploded through her, taking her breath as stars exploded behind her closed eyes. She panted his name over and over as he took a few more draws of her blood then licked the wound closed.

It was her turn.

Lowering her head, she yanked the collar of his shirt to the side and slammed her fangs in to the muscle there. He yelled with release as she took strong pulls of his blood, bringing him in to herself as he had with her. Their essence mingled, their souls, for just a moment, becoming one.

As Dannon twitched beneath her with his aftershocks, Flora pulled from his shoulder and lapped at the droplets of blood there, closing the holes she'd created. His arms wrapped around her back and hugged her to his chest tightly, his chin resting on her shoulder as they both struggled to catch their breath.

Her phone chimed again and both Flora and Dannon cursed, then snorted at their mutual reaction. Flora lifted from Dannon and scooted until her feet were on the ground. Still naked, Flora bent and sifted through her clothes until she located her phone and brought it to life. "Damn it," she muttered.

"What now?" Dannon asked, tucking himself in to his pants as he pulled them up his legs.

"I don't know. Something's going on with John."

Dannon frowned up at her as she scooped her clothes from the floor and headed for the bedroom. No use getting dressed when she'd be going to bed soon, anyway. "He's pissed that we left."

"What did he say?"

"Told me that he thought it was shitty of me to push him away when he's always been there for me when I needed him. I think he's just drunk. Hopefully, the jackass doesn't try to drive home."

"I'll text Mattie and tell him to keep an eye on him. Make sure he gets an uber."

Flora dropped her clothes in to the hamper and pulled out a clean pair of panties and a tank top before heading for the shower. She hated to wash Dannon's scent from her, but it had been a hot and humid day and she officially felt sticky.

Keeping the water a little on the cooler side, Flora tipped her head back and let the water run over her hair and down her back. Dannon's footsteps echoed down the hall and stopped in front of the bathtub. "What?" she called out, not bothering to open her eyes.

"Mattie said Joe already left but he doesn't know whether he drove himself or not."

"Great," Flora grumbled. The last thing she wanted was for her friend to get suspended for getting a DUI after hanging out with Flora for the night. "I'm going to kick his ass tomorrow."

"Is he coming by?"

Flora shrugged, then remembered Dannon had never opened the curtain. "I don't know. I'm pretty much out of the office until we can figure out who's behind this shit. If I go in, you have to be on my arm. Chief's orders."

"Can we just stay in bed until the case is solved?"

140

"That just sounded so bad sitcom-ish." Flora laughed and then rinsed off. Pulling the curtain back, she took the towel from Dannon's outstretched hand as his eyes roamed her body from head to toe.

"I'd rather lick the water off," Dannon said, his voice that deep growly sound that said he was ready for round two.

Dropping the towel on to the ground, she dipped her chin and looked up at him through her lashes. "So, what are you waiting for?"

Dannon carried Flora in to the bedroom where they made love three more times before letting sleep consume them. And, for once, she slept soundly, no sounds of cars outside on the street to constantly wake her.

"Flora," a voice whispered in the dark, invading her dreams. She groaned and rolled over, wanting more sleep. "Flora, wake up."

Eyes flying open, Flora sat straight up in the bed when she spotted Tomas on the other side of the bed, a gun pointed at Dannon's temple. Her mate stared straight up at the ceiling. The only evidence he was even still alive was his Adam's apple bobbing low as he swallowed hard.

"Tomas," Flora said, slowly rolling off the side of the bed, her hands raised, palms out, as she pulled her eyes from Dannon to level them on Kian's asshole guard. "What the hell are you doing?"

"Get dressed, sunshine."

What the fuck was he doing there? Did that mean they were right about Kian the whole time? Flora moved toward her dresser. Maybe if she could distract him, she could grab her own gun from inside her underwear drawer.

"Ah ah," Tomas said, pushing the muzzle further against Dannon's temple, pushing his head a little. "I laid your clothes out. Keep your fucking hands out of that drawer."

Did that mean Tomas knew where she hid her gun? Had he gone through her drawers before? What a creepy fucking feeling. First, with someone taking pics of her while she was in the throes of passion and sending them to the fucking vampire Prince. Now, this prick had rifled through her shit while she'd been out?

Grabbing the clothes Tomas indicated to with a jerk of his chin, Flora slowly pulled everything in to place, trying to form some kind of plan in her head as she watched how incredibly steady Tomas's hand was. "Did Kian send you? Is he worried we'll turn him over to the Executioner?" she asked as he held a fucking firearm to her mate's head. And she'd bet everything she owned those were silver bullets loading that magazine.

He chuckled softly, shaking his head slowly. "No, dumbass."

Then why else would he be there? What could he possibly have to gain by this? "Tell me what's going on. Why are you here?"

Shit. Think, Flora. There had to be some way to get him away from Dannon enough for him to take the fucker down. She could take him down, but she feared if she even feinted in his direction, Tomas would pull the trigger.

"I thought you were so fucking smart, Flora. Don't you have it figured out yet?"

She frowned at him. Figured what out yet? They'd thought Kian was the asshole who'd set Dannon up, but things hadn't added up. Was he saying she'd been right the first time?

"Drawing a blank here," she said, crossing her arms over his chest. "If you're pissed at me for kicking your ass, put the fucking gun on me. Take it off Dannon's head." She'd give up her life in a heartbeat if it meant Dannon would go on. If it meant he'd still walk this planet.

"Yeah. I'll take it off his head so he can jump me. Don't fucking think so." He shook his head. "And you didn't kick my ass, bitch. I'm pretty sure I remember your ass being on the ground, not me."

Good; she'd hit a nerve. High emotions always caused mistakes. He just had to make one and she'd take the fucker down. "Then tell me why the fuck you're here."

Tomas shook his head. "Yeah. I'll just be a movie villain and spill my guts to you."

"Then we're at a standstill. Because unless you tell me what you want, I can't help you."

He barked out a laugh, his eyes not matching the soulless smile on his lips. "I don't need your fucking help, you dumb cunt."

Okay. Now he was pissing her off. "Then what the fuck do you want, you fucking jackass?"

Wrong thing to say.

When the gun went off, Flora's heart stopped. It literally stopped in her chest and her soul screamed in agony. As the ringing in her ears drowned everything out, she turned her eyes to the bed, praying with everything she had that her man's brains weren't splattered all over her sheets.

Chapter Thirteen

Dannon's eyes were squeezed shut and there was a rather large hole in her pillow lying beside him. But he was alive. He was still breathing.

"Fuck!" Flora yelled. "Tell me what you want so we can get this over with. If you're pissed at me about something, then fucking shoot me. But stop pointing that thing at his fucking head."

Maybe she should've kept her mouth shut, but her beast was screaming inside of her head, ready to burst through and push any conscious thought Flora might have to the darkest recesses of her mind. She wanted to kill Tomas, wanted to rip his head from his shoulders, but even in her True Form, that didn't mean she'd be faster than a bullet.

"I want what's mine, you stupid bitch!" Tomas yelled back.

That stopped any retort Flora might have had, any smart-ass comments she might have slung at him. He wanted what was his? What the fuck did that mean? She'd never taken anything from him.

"What?" she muttered, her brows low, her face scrunched in confusion.

"The second Kian is nailed on the humans' murders and a cop's murder, he'll be taken out and left for the sun. And guess what happens after that?"

Putting her fingertips to her temples, Flora lowered her gaze to Dannon. No fucking way. "You're next in line."

"Ding ding ding."

"Thought you weren't going to be the stupid villain and spill your guts," Flora said, goading him. Why couldn't she keep her fucking mouth shut? "You're forgetting something. You're not the right bloodline. I'm sure there's someone else in his family who'll step up once the Prince is dead."

"And that's where you're wrong. Maybe you should study up on other species other than your own. You know, since you're supposed to be the law and all," he said. "I'm Head Guard. If the

Prince dies, I'm the one who steps in his place. And once the fucking Queen is gone, I'm King." His chest poked out as if he were proud of himself for coming up with this plan.

"You forget the Queen will live just as long as you. Once she finds out you got her son killed, she'll make sure you suffer for eternity. And she will find out. I got close, Tomas. Maybe I didn't peg you specifically, but I got close."

Flora led the way out of the room with Dannon following close behind. She wanted to reach back and take his hand, but Tomas would probably shoot a hole in her wall next. Or at least she hoped he'd give another warning. So, instead, she moved in to the living room and sat on the sofa, Dannon lowering beside her.

"If you're here just to kill us, why all the theatrics? Why didn't you just put a bullet in our brains while we slept?"

"Because then it'll look like someone broke in and murdered you. Nope. I have better plans than that. More fun plans. I borrowed your phone. Is that okay?" He raised his brows as if he were truly asking permission, but then smiled as he brought her phone to life and hit the screen over and over.

"Who are you texting?" Flora asked, still at a loss as to how to get them out of this. Why didn't she hide guns throughout her house like Dannon did? She was a fucking cop; shouldn't she have more than one at hand?

"Your new boyfriend," Tomas said with a grin.

So he'd sent the pics. But how the hell had he gotten hold of them? She still didn't even know who'd taken them. "Where'd you get the pictures?" she asked.

Tomas slowly folded in to the armchair across from her and Dannon, the muzzle still pointed at Dannon. Fuck. Why wouldn't he turn it away from her mate? Why did he see Dannon as a bigger threat when she was the one with the fucking badge? Flora glanced at Dannon. Oh, that's why.

His humanoid façade was gone completely, his eyes blazing bright gold, his cheeks sharp, his wings present, his muscles taut as a sneer seemed permanently planted on his lips. "Calm down," Flora whispered, reaching for his hand.

"Nope. Sit still. Unless you want to see what silver does to your man," Tomas said, chuckling at his own joke.

"I'm going to kill you," Dannon growled, his voice so deep and growly, all semblance of human was gone. Ooooh. He was so close to losing complete control over his demon. While Flora was tempted to tell him to unleash hell, she wasn't sure either of them could move fast enough to avoid getting a bullet to the brain or heart.

"Yeah. I can see that," Tomas said, his tone bored as he leaned back and crossed an ankle over his knee and rested the gun on his thigh, still pointed at Dannon.

If she could just distract him somehow.

They sat like that, in silence other than the constant growl that trickled up Dannon's throat, for a while. It could've been ten minutes, it could've been thirty. She had no way of knowing since she didn't own a clock and her phone was in Tomas's possession.

There was a sharp knock on the door. Just three taps. Tomas smiled and gestured them both up with a wave of his gun.

"Fuck you. Get it yourself," Dannon growled out.

Tomas's smile faded and he slowly rose, crossed the room, then shoved the gun under Flora's chin, forcing her head back at an odd angle. Fuck. Maybe he wasn't bluffing.

"Get that fucking away from her," Dannon said, his body tensing as he turned to look at her.

"I'm going to count to three and then her brains will be all over the wall back there."

Dannon's growl deepened. "Get the fuck away from her."

"One..."

"Fuck," Dannon growled out, slowly lifting from his spot beside Flora.

Tomas used the muzzle of the gun to force Flora to her feet. If Dannon didn't kill him, Flora would. This son of a bitch needed to die, and painfully.

Dannon backed toward the front door, his eyes on Tomas and Flora, that growl growing louder by the second. "Growl all you want, demon. The results won't change." His words might have sounded confident, but Flora could hear the slight tremor, could sense the fear and trepidation pouring from him. He'd gone too far to turn back now and he knew it. If he didn't kill both of them, he'd lose. Either one of them would rip him to pieces or the Executioner would take him out. Either way, he was a walking dead man.

"Go ahead and answer that," Tomas said, barely turning his head to look at Dannon, the gun still jammed against the soft flesh under Flora's jaw.

With one loud growl, Dannon stepped backward and yanked the door open. Tomas kept himself and Flora just out of sight, watching Dannon from the corner of the wall.

"Hey," Kian's voice greeted. His voice sounded confused, and Flora could just imagine the frown creating a crease between his brows. "Flora texted me. Told me to come over immediately. Said she needed help." There was a beat of silence. Then Kian's voice deepened and a snarl tainted his words. "What the fuck did you do to her?"

Dannon's growl softened, but he didn't say a word. Just stepped back so Kian could enter the house. Kian passed by Flora without noticing her at first. When he turned back to say something to Dannon, his eyes landed on her and his words were cut off with a gasp.

"What the fuck are you doing?" Kian said, every word growing louder as his eyes moved from Dannon, to Flora, to the gun shoved against her chin. "Get away from her. I told you, she's not to be touched. What fucking part of that didn't you understand?"

"Shut the fuck up and have a seat," Tomas said, that tiny tremor still there in his voice. Yeah; he was nervous. Dannon and Flora were already far stronger than he was; now his own Prince had been thrown in to the equation. Three against one were terrible odds for him. And he knew it. If he didn't maintain the upper hand, he'd be dropped in a heartbeat.

Kian's brows were pulled so low it created a shadow as he lowered his chin and glared at his Second in command. Red flashed behind his irises as his fangs dropped from his gums. He turned that glare on Dannon. "Is this because of what we did?"

"I have nothing to do with this," Dannon said, his growl finally fading to almost nothing. His eyes left Flora for only a second to glance at Kian before turning his attention back to her. It was like he was afraid if he looked away from her, she'd either disappear or Tomas would pull the trigger.

"What are you doing, Tomas?" Kian asked, slowly moving further in to the room and taking a couple of steps in his direction.

"I said sit the fuck down. Or do you want to be the one responsible for her death?" Tomas shoved the gun harder against her chin and Flora actually cried out in pain. Son of a bitch. That shit hurt.

"Fuck, stop. We're sitting," Dannon said, throwing his hands up, palms out, as he inched sideways back to the couch. When Kian didn't make a move, Dannon reached out and wrapped a hand around his bicep, dragging him with him.

Both men sat and Tomas finally pulled the gun away from her head. With a hard shove, Tomas pushed Flora toward the couch and the two men who looked like they were ready to shred Tomas with their bare hands. She stumbled, but righted herself before she face planted on to the hardwood floor. How had he even gotten in here? She kept the fucking place locked tight. Had someone given him a key or something? And who? The only other person who had a key was...

"Joe," Flora breathed out.

Tomas whipped around, expecting him to be standing behind him. When he turned back, his scowl was deeper.

"What about him?" Dannon asked.

"He's the only one I can think of that would've taken the pictures and has a key to my house. Hell. I haven't even given you one, yet."

"You gave your fuck buddy a key to your house but not your mate?" Tomas asked, a bark of a laugh bursting from his lips. "That's fucking awesome."

"I've known Joe for years."

"Yeah, okay. Whatever."

With this asshole rubbing it in Dannon's face, Flora did feel a little shitty for a second. But her and Dannon were almost always together. So far, she'd had no reason to make a copy for him. Not that she wouldn't. As soon as this shit was over, she planned on taking her happy ass down to the hardware store and getting him keys made to her house, her car, anything she owned.

If they got through this alive.

The front door of her house opened and her heart jumped. Maybe someone had figured out what was going on. Maybe someone had followed the Prince to her house and worried when he didn't make contact.

Except this wasn't a movie or some bad cop show.

Instead of backup or help of some kind, in walked the one and only Candy, the same bitch from Dannon's club.

"What the hell are you doing here?" Dannon asked.

"I thought you wanted me here," she said, her brows furrowed. "Wasn't getting rid of her part of your plan?"

Dannon didn't say a word; his head turned slowly to look at Flora. No way. No way could Dannon be behind this entire thing. No way could he have come up with some stupid ass scheme just to kill her. No way would Dannon work with Tomas to get rid of Kian, no matter how much he hated the vamp. He loved her…didn't he?

"I thought you said once she was out of the way we could pin the murders on her and be together?" Candy said, true emotion in her voice as she slowly walked closer to Tomas's side.

"What the fuck is she talking about, Dannon?" Flora asked, her wings bursting free from her back and flexing past the holes of her tank top as rage burned a path through her system. Her demon was so close to the surface, so close to fully taking over her body she could barely think straight.

"Look at me," he said, his voice deep. Flora slowly turned her head to glare at the man who'd stolen her heart. And now that fucking organ was shattering. "You know she's full of shit. You know the bitch is lying."

"Dannon," Candy gasped, her hand going to her chest. "You can drop the act now."

Tomas chuckled softly as she sat on the arm of the chair beside where he stood.

"Do you really think I'd want anything to do with you after all this bullshit?"

Candy's frown smoothed and she giggled. "What makes you think there will be an after for you?"

"Why the fuck are you even here?" Flora asked, anger sending fire through her veins as he stomach tightened with adrenaline.

"Well, since you didn't want to be Queen, I get to take your place."

"Tomas," Kian said, leaning forward, his elbows resting on his knees. "What are you doing?"

Tomas's eyes turned and leveled on Kian. "You weak fuck." Kian tensed beside Flora. "Chasing after our fucking enemy as your Queen? Are you fucking kidding me? This bastard disrespects you every chance he gets and what do you do? Nothing. You have me beat for punishing that bitch for her insubordinance."

So, Kian really did have Tomas punished for laying his hands on her.

"She's a cop. And a woman. You know damn well that's against not just their laws, but ours. We don't hurt women."

"No, you don't hurt women. We're superior to those fucking perverts. Yet, you chased after her like a fucking dog in heat."

"He plans on killing you and us and pinning all of the murders on us. But, how do you plan on explaining away our deaths?" Flora asked. She rolled her shoulders, trying to ease the discomfort of her shirt pinning the base of her wings to her back.

"I killed you while trying to protect my Prince," Tomas said with a shrug. Well shit. Guess he had thought all of this through.

A soft thud sounded from outside of the west window. All eyes turned that way before Tomas quickly returned his attention to his hostages. "Go check that out," he told Candy.

"Hell no. I'm fucking human. What if it's another one of them?"

"It's the middle of the night, you dumb bitch. No one knows we're here."

"Nope. Still not going out there." She crossed her arms over her chest. Well, there definitely wasn't any love or affection between the two of them. Guess their bond was based on nothing more than their mutual psychotic tendencies.

"You realize you're fired," Dannon said, his voice deep but his tone level. Flora snorted a laugh; she couldn't help herself. Of all the things going through Dannon's mind right now, that was the first one he focused on.

"Kill them both. Fuck him. He wasn't even that great of a fuck, anyway," Candy said, crossing her arms over her chest. She was doubling down on her earlier attempts at putting some kind of riff between Flora and Dannon. It wouldn't work.

"For fuck's sake," Dannon said, lunging to his feet and stalking toward Candy. Tomas followed him with the gun but didn't move or tell him to stop. Keep going, Dannon. Just a little further. Keep his eyes on you. "We never had sex. You can pretend all you want, but don't you think I'd be honest if we had? It's no secret the kind of life we live." He continued to stalk her and she took two steps back. Come on, Dannon. Just a little more.

"Did you help him kill those men? Is that how the cops knew they were at my club, because you told him? What did you do? Text him and tell him every time you thought there might be an altercation?"

"Who cares about those assholes? They were fucking perverts," Candy whined, but she was still stepping away from Dannon, the bravado slipping. "I'm too small to kill anyone." Her eyes flitted to Tomas then back. "Tomas, make him stop."

"Wait a second," Tomas said, fully turning his whole body, his gun still pointed toward Dannon, but now it was low enough that, even if he shot her mate, it might not kill him. Not if they could get him help fast enough to get the silver out of his system before it poisoned him. "All I did was take pictures and help your little ass hide the bodies. Don't try to put it all on me."

Tomas hadn't killed them? Candy had? How? She was smaller than Flora and human.

"Oh, don't look so surprised," Candy said when she caught Flora's disbelieving look. "It's not too hard to lure someone in to a secluded area when all they have on their mind is raping you. Stupid fucks just didn't think someone would finally fight back. Guess they should've checked for weapons before forcing me to my knees." She giggled, the sound maniacal.

"How did you know who they were?" Flora asked, mentally cursing herself for bringing any attention to herself when she needed Tomas distracted enough for her to take him out.

"I invited them. They're all fucking registered, remember? Wasn't all that hard to track the sick fucks down. And look at me," she said, holding her arms wide. "I might be legal, but I look young enough they all thought they'd get to rape a kid. Fuck them. I'm glad they're dead."

Flora couldn't argue with that, but there were laws. She would have to face the same consequences for murder as the others. She'd still have to answer to a judge and spend time in jail. Hell. For as many men as she'd killed, she'd probably never see the light of day again.

Tomas was slowly stalking further away from Flora, forcing him to either turn his back on Flora or Dannon. He caught on, his head turning to check on Flora, but she remained seated beside Kian in hopes of keeping his attention on Dannon. If he thought Dannon the bigger threat, he'd ignore her long enough for her to actually do something.

"Stop following me," Candy said as Dannon backed her in to a wall. She whimpered as Dannon's wings flexed, spanning a couple of feet from either side. He was beautiful, but Flora knew without looking at him that his fangs had elongated and his eyes were blazing bright, not to mention the sharp edge of his cheekbones. What she found stunning, Candy found terrifying.

Flora was still confused as to why exactly she'd tried to throw Dannon under the bus; exactly what she thought she'd gain from any of this. But if she opened her mouth again, it would pull Tomas's attention back to her.

As Tomas and Candy both focused on Dannon, Flora let her true form to the surface, pushing her demon just far enough back so it couldn't take full control, and slowly rose to her feet. She only had about two yards between her and Tomas. As long as he didn't turn around, she could make it, disarm the fucker, and get some backup before either she or Dannon lost control and shred both of these assholes to pieces. She really didn't want to have to replace furniture because it was stained with their blood. Not to mention, she'd probably get in a shit ton of trouble for killing a human.

Candy's eyes were lifted to Dannon's face. Flora watched Tomas's back as she crept across the floor, stepping around the coffee table. Her movement caught Candy's attention. "No!" she cried out as Flora lunged for Tomas.

Arm whipping around, Tomas's head swung around, his eyes wide as Flora reached for him. A roar sounded a half second before the pop of Joe's gun erupted. And then there was pain. So much pain.

Something burned a path from her shoulder straight to every fucking cell in her body. Her nerve endings felt like they were on fire. And then her vision began to fade inward as the room swayed around her.

Another roar rattled the room as a black veil covered her vision and the room went silent. She'd underestimated Tomas. She'd overestimated her ability to fight off the effects of the silver singeing every living organ in her body.

She couldn't even open her mouth to tell Dannon how sorry she was. Or to say goodbye.

Chapter Fourteen

They were in tune, as much as any mated couple could be. Dannon knew the second he pulled Tomas's attention away, Flora would make a move. It was her job. She was a cop and had a lot more training than he had. He just hoped Kian would keep his royal ass planted on the couch and stay out of the way.

He also knew she was doing everything she could to keep the gun on her and off him. His selfless woman. But there was no chance he'd let Tomas aim that fucking thing at her. Not if he had a choice. As long as the muzzle was on Dannon, Flora was safe from the silver in those bullets.

When Candy had noticed Flora on the move and called out, Dannon only had a second to react. As he turned, he watched as if in slow motion as Tomas turned to see Flora coming for him and turned the gun on her.

Dannon jumped at him, hitting his arm and lowering the gun before he put a bullet between his mate's eyes.

But he'd been too fucking late.

His heart stuttered as he watched the blood bloom and then spill over from her shoulder as the bullet buried itself in her body. There was no spray behind her; she was being poisoned as he watched.

A roar ripped from him and then he could barely think straight. His demon, that monster they all carried, that same beast they fed on a regular basis to keep calm burst from him and pushed Dannon to the back. He could still see, still hear and feel, but he was no longer in control of his own fucking body.

Candy was tossed to the side like a ragdoll as Dannon ran for his woman, catching her as she crumpled to the floor. Kian jumped from the couch and took Tomas down, a battle cry ripping from his lips. He'd never seen the Prince behave in anything other than a formal manner. This guy was a brawler, much more feral than Dannon had ever thought possible.

154

There were dull thuds, a moan that cut off abruptly, then silence.

Dannon lifted his head and roared again as Flora's eyes rolled shut.

The front door exploded inward, the sound of wood crashing against the walls echoing through the house. Dannon didn't look up— couldn't look away from his heart, his love, his soul mate.

Joe's voice. A female. Another male. There was yelling, someone was barking orders.

Dannon couldn't focus on what Joe was saying. It didn't matter. All that mattered was the woman in his arms. The woman whose skin was far too pale, far too cool to the touch. She was dying.

"I'm going to kill that mother fucker," Dannon growled, all semblance of his human façade gone.

"Too late," Joe said, kneeling beside Dannon and Flora. His face was pale, his eyes rimmed with moisture as he stared down at Flora. Dannon knew how much Joe cared for her, but he wouldn't let anyone touch her. He couldn't.

It seemed like just yesterday this woman was parked outside of his house, watching him, following his every move. He'd been infatuated with her from the moment he'd sensed her out there, had watched her through the blinds as she leaned her head back against the seat and huffed in frustration.

Even then, he knew she'd be his.

He'd only had her a short time and now he'd lose her. If she died, he'd follow. There was no way he could go on as a shell. Not after he'd finally found her. Not after she'd rounded out all the jagged pieces to his puzzle. She made him feel real, made him want to be a good man, made him want to give her everything in the world just to see her smile.

Her breath hitched and she trembled. No. He wasn't giving up on her. Not yet. He couldn't. He couldn't imagine this beautiful woman no longer in existence.

"Would my blood help?" Kian said, standing just behind Dannon.

"No. Your blood is no different to us than anyone else," Jane, Flora's boss and friend said, kneeling on Flora's other side. She lifted her eyelid, leaned down to listen to her heart, her breathing. "Help's coming, Flora. Just hang on, girl."

"Where the fuck are they?" Dannon growled out, finally lifting his eyes to Joe's.

The son of a bitch's eyes were red rimmed and moisture clung to his cheeks.

"I texted her to apologize for being a prick. She didn't answer. She always answers. When I got here...I should've come in sooner."

That had been him outside. Shit. Why hadn't he just crashed in to the house? Why had he waited?

But he couldn't blame Joe. Couldn't blame anyone but himself for being so careless. He should've heard Tomas entering the house. He should've...

Flora shouldn't be lying on the floor dying. That bullet was meant for him. Had he just kept Tomas's attention, Flora would be fine. She wouldn't be fading right there in his arms.

The need to kill something or someone was beginning to override all other thought. His demon wanted revenge. Wanted to bleed someone for this crime.

Dannon fought to the front, needing to think clearly and he couldn't do that when all the demon saw was red through its fury.

Candy moaned and whimpered from somewhere behind him, but he didn't bother looking back at her. She might have been human, but his demon wanted to rip her head from her shoulders just as much as Tomas's. The fucker might already be dead, but that didn't assuage the violence his demon needed to commit. This was just as much her fault.

"Why, Candy?" he asked.

Rustling fabric, another whimper.

"Answer me. Why?"

"I wanted to be Queen," she whined, her voice forced as if she were in pain. Good.

"You killed men, humans, pinned it on me, planned to kill my mate, and thought what...once the Prince was dead, his people would just bow at your feet? You're lucky you're still alive, you psycho fucking bitch."

Sirens met his sensitive ears and hope bloomed. There might still be time. He had no idea how far the silver had worked through her system. If it'd already gone to her heart or brain. If it had...

Joe rushed to the front door and then heavy steps followed him back. Hands pulled at Dannon, but he just growled deeper, louder.

"You've got to move so they can help her," Kian said, crouching beside him, his hand on Dannon's shoulder. He'd much rather snap that hand from his wrist than move from Flora's side.

"Come on, man. Let them help her," Joe said from his other side.

As a tear streaked down his cheek, Dannon slid out from under her and moved just enough for the paramedics to work on her. Since the emergence of all the others, all paramedics had to have at least one non-human on the ambulance at all times. Flora's system wasn't like a human's and would require different care.

He just prayed that they'd get her back to his arms.

As he watched them check her, watched them load her on to a stretcher and rush her from the house, Dannon already started making plans of how he'd die the second Flora's heart stopped beating.

Chapter Fifteen

Flora's dream faded as noise infiltrated her ears. Too loud. Her eyelids fluttered open…too bright. She felt like she'd been hit by a Mack truck and then had it back up over and over, continuously running her over before someone finally set her on fire.

Everything hurt. Everything burned. Just opening her eyes took too much effort.

Something was beeping to her left. Her hand was wrapped in something warm and kind of hard. There was a weight across her legs. She shifted and could move, but again, that small movement felt like she'd run a marathon.

Attempting to open her eyes again, she struggled to focus. She was in a white room, no lights were on overhead, but the window to her right was bare. And someone was stretched out on an uncomfortable looking chair beneath it. Her hand was clasped in Dannon's, his head laying on his forearm, his other arm stretched across her thighs. That had been the weight. Dannon was holding her the only way he could.

Raising the hand not trapped by her mate, she groaned as the movement sent more pain pinging through her system. Fuck. Through everything she'd done, everything she'd endured, she'd never felt pain like this. What was causing the agony ripping her apart?

Scenes from her house began to play in rapid succession. Tomas with a gun pointed at Dannon. Tomas's stupid plan to take over the throne. Candy. Kian. A gunshot.

Turning her head, Flora tucked her chin to get a look at her shoulder. It was bandaged heavily. That mother fucker had shot her. She'd been poisoned with silver. And she was still alive.

Shifting again, she groaned as another wave of pain hit her. She was kind of alive. She definitely felt like shit. Damn. What kind of damage had the silver done to her system to have every neve ending firing off like this?

"Flora?" a hoarse voice said, the tone filled with disbelief.

Turning her head, she found Joe sitting up, propping himself on his elbow, his eyes wide, his lips parted as he stared at her.

"Hi," she said, her throat burning with the effort.

"Dannon," Joe said. Then louder, he called out to her mate still sleeping beside her. "Dannon, wake the fuck up."

Flora winced from the sound. It felt like someone had taken a sledgehammer directly to her skull.

Dannon's hand tightened around hers as he sighed a mixture of a breath and a groan. Turning his head more, his lids fluttered open, closed, then popped back open when he spotted Flora watching him. His head lifted quickly, his body went straight, and the jostling movement sent more pain raging through her system.

"Flora? Are you awake?" he asked. What a silly question. She was looking right at him. "Do you know where you are? Do you know who I am?"

Flora frowned at him, glanced at Joe with raised brows then turned her gaze back to Dannon. "Apparently, I'm in the hospital. And you're my mate. Yeah, I'm awake. Although, I'd rather still be asleep." Hell. She'd pay someone to knock her out right about now just to escape the pain.

"Holy shit," Joe breathed out then lunged to his feet. He was out the door before Flora had a chance to ask what he was doing.

"Do you remember everything? Do you feel okay?"

Flora frowned down at Dannon. "Yeah. Of course I remember everything. And no, I don't feel okay. I hurt. Bad. What the hell did they do?"

Dannon released a rush of air and dropped his head to her chest, a silent sob shaking his body once. "Hey," Flora said, raising her arm to run her fingers through his hair and ignoring the sharp pain the movement caused. "I'm okay. We're okay."

His voice was thick when he finally spoke. "They said they didn't know if you were going to make it. The silver…" His voice hitched. "The silver had worked its way through your entire body. They didn't know if it'd done any damage to your brain or heart."

It felt like she'd been out for a few minutes, but that obviously wasn't the case. "How long have I been…"

"Four days." Dannon raised his head. Tears stained his cheeks and welled in his eyes. "And they couldn't find any brain activity in that time. They didn't know if you were a vegetable or if you would just die overnight."

Wow. She'd been that close to leaving Dannon forever. That was probably why she didn't realize she'd been out so long. She hadn't even dreamed according to Dannon and the doctors. "Four days?" she breathed out, trying to wrap her mind around how close she'd come to dying.

Joe hurried back in, a doctor and nurse on his heels. "See? I told you," he said, as if someone had thought he'd been lying.

"Miss Grumio, I'm Dr. Tair," she said, stepping to the side of the bed and checking the monitors Flora was hooked to. There were wires coming from all over her body, her head, her chest, a little clamp on her finger. "How do you feel?"

"Like someone took a sledgehammer to every part of my body."

The nurse was busy checking the bag hanging near Flora's head, her hand sliding down the line to check where it was poking in to her arm. A small smile lifted the corners of her lips at Flora's words. "But you're alive," she said without looking at Flora.

"Do you know where you are? Do you know your name?" Dr. Tair asked.

"We already went through all that," Dannon said. "She remembers."

"What happened exactly? Why am I alive?" Not that she wasn't grateful, but as her consciousness was fading, she truly believed it was too late. That there had been too much silver in her system for any life saving measures.

"You're lucky," Dr. Tair said, no longer staring at the monitors, but directly in to Flora's eyes. There was a faint glow. Just enough for Flora to know the doctor wasn't a human. "They got you here in time. Ten more minutes, fifteen tops, and you would be lost. Your people care a lot about you."

Wow. So close. "Thank you," Flora said, although she wasn't exactly sure for what part.

Joe and the doctor moved a little away from the bed and were engaged in a somewhat heated conversation. Joe wanted her released, the doctor adamantly refused. But all Flora could focus on was the feeling of Dannon's fingers gently stroking up and down the arm not attacked to some machine. His eyes were on her face, those tears still shimmering in their brown depths. He'd thought he'd lost her, and, by the way he was staring at her, refused to look away lest she vanish. But she was here. She was alive. And she really wanted to kick someone's ass for making her body hurt this badly.

"Where's Tomas?" He was first on her list. Candy was a close second. Oh, how nice it would be to have them both in the same fucking room…

"Dead," Dannon said, his voice still thick with the emotion he was trying to hold in.

"Who killed him?"

"Kian." A feral smile was on his soft lips now. She needed him to smile, she needed him to realize she was fine, they were both okay, they were safe and together, and now there was no more bull shit for them to worry about.

"Really?" Huh. They'd seriously pegged the Prince all wrong. "Candy?"

"Currently sitting in jail. She'll have to face the human courts, though, so no Executioner."

"Shame," she said, leaning her head back against the pillow and staring at the ceiling. Honestly, she'd rather be the one to take Candy out then let the courts kill her. She wanted to choke the bitch out with her bare hands for what she'd put them through. "How's Kian doing?"

He'd killed his Head Guard after the fucker tried to pin the murders on him. How fucked up.

"He's trying to keep up that arrogant act, but he's pretty torn up. He trusted Tomas. And he's blaming himself for you getting shot."

The last few words were spoken through clenched teeth. "You can't seriously be jealous," Flora said, rolling her head on her pillow to look at her mate.

"It's going to take a little longer than a few days to get over the fact that vamp was trying to steal my wife," Dannon said, lowering his head to press a kiss to Flora's knuckles, his lips so soft and gentle. "He's been trying to get in here."

Flora frowned. "You didn't let him?"

With a slow shake of his head, Dannon raised his eyes to her face. "I didn't know if I was going to lose you. And, as stupid as it sounds, I kind of blame him for this as much as he does. It was his fucking Guard who did this."

"His Guard. Not him. You said he killed Tomas. He didn't have to."

Dannon continued to stare up at Flora, his eyes bouncing between hers. "Maybe later," he said. "I want you to myself for now."

Flora snorted, then winced with the pain. "How long is this shit supposed to hurt?"

The doctor hesitated as she walked to the door after arguing with Joe. "You might be okay in a couple of days, or it might take a month. Maybe you can convince your buddy that you need to stay so I can keep an eye on you." She sneered at Joe, turned on her heel, and left with the nurse trailing after her.

"I don't want her to leave yet," Dannon said, not bothering to look up at Joe.

"I don't want her here. Unless you plan on staying twenty-four/seven. It's too fucking open."

"Did you really think I was going to leave until she was ready to go home?" Dannon asked, finally peeling his gaze from Flora to cock a brow at Joe. "Go home, Joe. You look like shit."

"Oh yeah, and you look a whole lot better." Joe threw a hand in the air, crossed the room, bent to place a kiss to Flora's temple, then smiled once before leaving her alone with her mate.

"I thought you said Tomas was dead?" Flora said, narrowing her eyes at Dannon.

"He is. Joe's just paranoid. He thinks the douche might have had someone other than Candy helping him. I doubt it, though. So does Kian."

Tears welled in Dannon's eyes again. "Now what?" She'd finally gotten him to calm down a little, or at least talk about something else.

"I just can't believe you're talking to me. The doctor really believed you were brain dead."

"What would you have done?" She'd never want Dannon to waste the rest of his life staying committed to her if she wasn't really there. The thought of him going through life alone, all the while grieving her even though she was right there, right in front of his eyes, broke her heart.

"I would've been right here." A tear spilled over his lashes and rolled down his cheek.

"I love you," she whispered. She'd never want that for him, but she knew there was no reason to argue with him about it or even talk about it anymore. That wouldn't happen. Not now. And as long as they still had time together, she'd cherish every second.

"I love you," he said, standing to press the softest brush of a kiss to her lips. "I love you so much."

Flora spent the next three weeks regaining her strength. It took two of those weeks just for the damn pain to go away. For a while, she'd actually contemplated drowning herself in booze and pain meds just to numb her body until she was fully healed. But, instead, she fought through it.

Now, she just wanted to get back to work, get back to chasing the bad guys. And she couldn't wait to sit in the courtroom and testify when Candy finally got taken before the judge. She still wanted to kill her or at least beat her to a bloody pulp for everything she and Tomas had put her and Dannon through.

Kian was on constant apology mode, sending flowers and treats daily. No matter how many times Flora said otherwise, Kian blamed himself for his Guard's behavior. He thought the fact he'd shown her so much attention was what caused Tomas to single her out to begin with. But Tomas was after Dannon long before she came in to the picture.

"What are you thinking about?" Dannon asked, leaning against the doorframe of her bedroom as she pulled her shoes on.

"Everything and nothing." She glanced up at him then did a double take. "What? What's going on now?"

"Why do you think something's wrong?"

"Because you look terrified and I can smell your fear from here."

"No you can't," he said with a chuckle, crossing the room to kneel in front of her.

"Maybe not, but you just admitted you were scared. What's wrong? What happened?"

Dannon took both of her hands in his and dropped his head. Shit. This couldn't be good if he couldn't even look her in the eye. When he raised his head, though, there was a sweet smile pulling up the corners of his lips. "We're not human."

With a frown, Flora raised one brow. "Yeah. I'm aware."

He laughed again and shook his head. "What I mean is, we bonded over almost months ago." Had it only been that long? It felt like she'd known him for years. "You're my mate for the rest of eternity, whether you like it or not."

"Romantic," she teased. Nothing like telling a girl she was tethered to you and there wasn't a damn thing you could do about it.

"We don't do ceremonies or anything like that. But after…" Dannon took a deep breath. Since she'd woken in the hospital, Dannon rarely left her side and treated her like she might disappear at any point, like she might blow away in the breeze. "I want to be connected to you in every way possible, and that includes in the human sense."

Flora narrowed her eyes at him. Shaking her head, she opened her mouth to ask him what he was talking about, but he pressed his fingers to her mouth and stopped her.

"Humans exchange rings. They have a ceremony and a party to let everyone know they're together. I want that with you. I want the entire world to know you belong to me and I belong to you. The

164

marks tell the others we're claimed, but I want even humans to know you're off the market." Flora released a soft burst of laugh. Wow. He wanted… "Marry me, Flora. Wear a pretty dress and get some flowers and let me put a ring on your finger."

"Dannon…" She didn't know what to say. What could she say except, "Yes. Of course." She'd tattoo his name across her chest if it would make him happy. That's all she wanted. She wanted him happy. She wanted him to feel how he made her feel every day. And she loved the thought of every species on this planet knowing she was his. "I would be honored to wear your ring."

Dannon's smile spread slowly, and widened until the corners of his eyes crinkled. His eyes flashed a bright amber as he quickly stood, wrapping his arms around her and taking her with him. He hugged her against his chest, his lips pressing kisses to her hairline, her temple, her cheek, then finally her lips where he lingered.

"I love you," he said. "And now the whole world will know how much."

The wedding was small and held in Flora's backyard. They only invited their closest friends and chose to have the party at her house, as well. There was no band, no DJ, no long, flowing white gown. But she did find a dress that caused Dannon's eyes to flash that beautiful color he got when his emotions were high. He was so handsome standing in front of her, clasping her hands as Jane read the words that would tie them together legally.

The party went well in to the night, everyone finally leaving shortly before the sun rose.

"Mrs. Michaels," Dannon said, lifting her with one arm under her knees and the other around her back.

"Wait. Why can't you take my last name?"

"Dannon Grumio?" he teased as he carried her through the house and in to the bedroom. They decided to sell his suburban home and live together in her isolated place where they could be themselves and stay in their True Form without fear of any neighbors seeing and freaking out about living next door to others.

"We could always hyphenate," Flora teased back.

Any other conversation was forgotten when his lips landed on hers. He had a way of doing that, of making her forget where she was or even who she was. It was more than just her body reacting to his; it was her heart and soul reaching for their mate.

Dannon and Flora made love three times before letting sleep claim them, then woke and went another two times before finally climbing out of bed. The urge to find someone else to feed from was no longer even an afterthought. They'd almost lost each other. She didn't want anyone else; didn't want to be with anyone else.

That didn't mean they couldn't still spend time at Club D when the situation arose. But now, they fed together. They fed from the lust in the room and took what they needed from each other's bodies. At least they did when a certain redhead wasn't at the club.